Girl with Fan

Twenty Short Stories

Phil Parker

Published in 2023 by FeedARead.com Publishing

Copyright © Phil Parker

The author or authors assert their moral right under the Copyright, Designs and Patents Act, 1988, to be identified as the author or authors of this work.

All Rights reserved. No part of this publication may be reproduced, copied, stored in a retrieval system, or transmitted, in any form or by any means, without the prior written consent of the copyright holder, nor be otherwise circulated in any form of binding or cover other than that in which it is published and without a similar condition being imposed on the subsequent purchaser.

A CIP catalogue record for this title is available from the British Library.

for Ann

Contents

The Self and Others

1. Ayesha — p7
2. Out of the Woods — p13
3. Patience — p24
4. Interludes — p32
5. The Missing Pages — p40
6. Pancake Day — p49
7. Alien Invasion — p60

The Arts Pages

8. Remember Me — p66
9. On the Canvas — p74
10. Girl with Fan — p82
11. UFO — p92
12. Out of Reach — p103
13. Green Shoots — p109
14. The Creative Impulse — p120

Amor Vincit Omnia – mostly...

15. Mistaken — p132
16. A Noise in the Night — p139
17. Over by Christmas — p149
18. Out of this World — p158
19. In the Deep Freeze — p164
20. The Night Shift — p173

Acknowledgements — p181

Ayesha

Ayesha stares at the reflection in the mirror and smiles. The reflection smiles back. This feels good. For some minutes there is careful scrutiny. It's not perfect – Ayesha has the wisdom to know this could not be true, given the current circumstances. But it will do. It will more than do. At last, after years of pretence, of trying to fit in, Ayesha has the sense that the image that stares back from the mirror's tarnished surface is something authentic, something real. It is the truth.

Mostly this comes from the new purchases, which arrived only this morning, and which Ayesha rushed back to the flat at the end of the morning shift to try on. It was awkward, of course. Ayesha defied anyone to put on a sari successfully the first time around. But now, after several false starts and much recourse to the explanations on the shop website, it seems possible to master the complex wrapping around the waist, the draping over the left shoulder, without the whole thing simply slithering to the ground. The petticoat purchased to wear underneath also feels both oddly new and curiously old-fashioned, but Ayesha experiences an inarticulate thrill in the whole ensemble. To wear the garments of one's ancestors, to step out in the garb that proclaims one's heritage, one's essential difference from the faceless crowds out on the streets – all this is more than special.

Ayesha spends several minutes staring at the mirror from a variety of angles. It would have been good to have had two mirrors, to have been able to place one directly behind as well as in front, so as to see the rear view also, but no matter. The purple silk feels so smooth, so cool, so light. It is almost erotic, Ayesha senses, but more than that, it is powerful. It is a statement. This is me, it says. It is who I am.

It has taken Ayesha more than a decade to get to this point. As an adopted child, there was a nagging sense of not really fitting in, even though Mother and Father had done their best to ensure that everyone knew that their new arrival was to be treated as a full part of the family. But difference haunted the details of the interaction in the small family home just as much as the more obvious, glaring contrasts. Ayesha knew even as a small child that when they were all out shopping in their tiny Norfolk town, tongues would wag, comments would be passed after they had traipsed out of the shop or wandered through the market square. Mum and Dad looked so different, as did cousins and uncles and aunts. Where they were stout, broad yeoman stock, Ayesha was elfin, delicate. Their ruddy complexions looked permanently weather-beaten beside Ayesha's smooth skin and finely-chiselled features. They ploughed the fields and chased rabbits with dogs. Ayesha dreamed of far-away worlds, exotic landscapes peopled by princes and emperors who rode not wheezing nags bogged down in East Anglian mud but elephants.

It was a kind household, Ayesha knew. There were no material needs. Ayesha had clothes – jeans, tee shirts, stout boots for family walks along the Norfolk coastline, sweatshirts emblazoned with names of rock bands, all in the rough and ready 'no airs and graces' fashion of the rest of the family. They even indulged Ayesha's odd passion for books. The bookshelf in the plainly functional bedroom Ayesha had been given from the earliest days was burdened down with tales of fantasy, poems about the Far East, versions of the Arabian Nights, as well as the more exotically inventive tales of other worlds and distant galaxies.

Now, in front of the mirror still, Ayesha smiles once more. So this is where the passion for dressing up would lead to. Memories stumble over each other in the fading light of the bedsit afternoon. Ayesha thinks of the early days at the local primary school, of being introduced as the new person who had come to join the class, who everyone should be nice to and invite to join in their play. Some of the girls clearly listened to Miss Allsopp only until morning break, when they turned their backs on Ayesha and proceeded as though this new visitor were simply invisible. Others, though, were more welcoming, and allowed Ayesha to join with their passionate, vivid games of making friends and falling out, games that often crossed the boundary into real life.

What Ayesha loved more than anything in that first year was the dressing-up box. No doubt it would have been impossible to explain, if Miss Allsopp or anyone else had taken the trouble to ask but, Ayesha senses now, it must surely have been about escape, of inhabiting another world, in another time and another identity. Of course, in the end even the kind girls had had enough. You're not like us, they'd say. You don't belong with us. Go outside and play in the yard.

Ayesha bites a lip pensively. No, it would not be possible to point back to childhood schooldays as the happiest days of one's life. Subsequently, the successors to the kindly maternal Miss Allsopp each, in their various ways, encouraged Ayesha out of the melancholy gloom that pervaded each classroom in turn. Ayesha 'has a vivid interior life,' a school report might say, or 'has a solitary personality, and does not mix readily with the other children.' Miss Chappell, sharp and no-nonsense to the end, wrote on the last end-of-year report before the transition to secondary school, that 'this young person is looking for something, but clearly has not found it yet.'

Ayesha's smile returns. Well, whatever it was, it has certainly been found now. It is ironic, Ayesha thinks, that those secondary school years, so turbulent, so challenging, so downright vicious at times, should also have been the route to this fulfilment. At puberty, no doubt, the herd instinct kicks in, the desperate need not to stand out, not to have attention drawn to one's difference. Yet, at the same time, those years bring the opportunity for trying out roles, for playing with notions of identity as maturity beckons.

Looking back now, Ayesha reflects, it was quirky Mr. Parkinson, the more than eccentric English teacher, who opened the door to the present. It might not have been deliberate, but it worked nonetheless. He had an odd choice in class readers, favouring fantasy fiction of various eras, but it meant that after CS Lewis, Ursula Le Guin and the inevitable Tolkien, there was time spent in the rather arcane company of H Rider Haggard, reading *She*, and then the sequel, *Ayesha, the Return of She*. Ayesha was not given to notions of predestination, but reading this cocktail of Tibetan fantasy, Ancient Egyptian myth, evil sorcerers and the like brought into focus the character of Rider Haggard's Ayesha herself, shape-shifting, exotic, all-powerful. In moments of introspection, Ayesha recognised that the attraction of the fiction was at least as much the Pre-Raphaelite line drawings of the edition that Mr. Parkinson used as it was the character of the novel's heroine, but no matter: from now on, Ayesha thought, this was the object over which to fantasise, an alter ego one could inhabit, a full-colour persona to challenge the monochrome tedium of small town life.

It would be dishonest to say that the transition into Norfolk's equivalent of Rider Haggard's fictional Ayesha was easy and seamless, but gradually the world of the village in which Ayesha grew up extended. Adolescence brought exposure to city life – yes, only the sleepy cosmopolitanism of Norwich, but even this came with its own excitements. Ayesha found dress shops, market stalls, niche bookshops, and hesitant contact with like-minded individuals searching for an alternative to the white, Anglo-Saxon patriarchal monoculture in which Ayesha had grown up. It was occasionally a bumpy ride – too many memories of being chased down back streets and alley ways by groups of youths with shaven heads and thick military boots. Once Ayesha inadvertently ended up enmeshed in an angry protest outside the City Hall and was told, at great length and in creatively violent language, to go home, to go back to wherever it was, that your sort just weren't wanted here.

It was internet shopping that provided both the solution to Ayesha's feelings of isolation and also, painfully, the trigger for the swift move out of the family home and into Ayesha's current, rather less than salubrious bedsit. Mother was initially intrigued by the parcels that arrived, but Ayesha was conscious that there was a limit to the number of times that these could be passed off as materials for an art project or a response to some school work on theatre make-up and costume design. With hindsight, it was clearly foolish not to have locked the bedroom door first, but when Mother wandered in just as Ayesha was putting the finishing touches to the most elaborate version yet of Rider Haggard's heroine – pastel pink salwar kameez with a vivid magenta chiffon veil, full face make up and blood-red painted nails – the initial silence was ominous. Mother curled her lip in distaste. When the words came, they were quiet, but wounded and angry.

'We've brought you up and cared for you since you were a tot. Fed you and clothed you. And is this how you repay us? To get yourself up looking like that? Get that lot off this minute and put your proper clothes on. What would your father say? I never want to see such a thing in this house again.'

Ayesha had expected tantrums and rages, rows and slammed doors. It was oddly nothing like that. The bedsit above the charity shop was available, Ayesha explained the plan matter-of-factly to Mother and Father, and within three weeks the move was made. At the end, there were even tears.

'We'll always love you, you know?' Mother said through her snuffles. 'No matter what … no matter what you wear or how you choose to go on.'

Ayesha was neither as happy as might have been imagined at all this freedom nor as sad as might have been feared at the loss of a family home. But in the weeks that followed, life in the bedsit brought its own comforts. After all, thought Ayesha, when you live on your own you get to be the person you want to be, to wear the clothes you want to wear, to live the life you want to live.

The phone rings. Ayesha steps back from the mirror, taking care not to trip over the hem of the sari, and picks it up. It's Mother. Ayesha sighs, prepares for whatever might come next, and taps the green icon to answer.

'Hi. Mum here. Is that you, Adrian?'

Ayesha sighs again. Baby steps. Life has to proceed very slowly. You can't rush people who won't be rushed. So, for now, it's Ayesha here in the security of the bedsit. The outside world might take a little more time.

'Hi, Mum,' he says.

Out of the Woods

As soon as I see her I know what's coming. Panic attacks almost always take the same path – my heart races, a feeling like waters rising inside me, as though my lungs will choke in their own fluid, and then tendrils like seaweed wrap around my throat. I'm drowning, and the hyperventilation only makes it worse. I lean forward, rest my head against the back of the pew in front of me, and will this to subside, but it doesn't. I have to get out.

I squeeze Dave's hand, offer a helpless smile, and murmur, 'Sorry. I have to go. Please.'

There's a moment of confusion as Dave's parents realize I'm going to push past them, and Dave's dad takes an age to stand up and let me out. I have to move, now.

'Sorry,' I say, as I push against him, 'sorry.'

Then, head down, hands clenched, I stumble back up the aisle, through a clutch of fussing bridesmaids clustered round the main door waiting for the bride, and out into the churchyard. The wind's fingers pull at my outfit. I grab my hat before it disappears over the hedge and into the field beyond, and slip out of sight behind the church. I find the nearest secluded gravestone, slump onto the marble slab and rest my forehead against the headstone. Slowly, painfully slowly, the waters drain away. Gradually I'm aware that someone is sobbing, and that the someone is me. I fumble around in my bag, rip open a pack of tissues, try to tidy myself up. After a while, the world rights itself again. I shiver, only partly because it's still just April and the clouds are scudding across the sky. Another deep breath, and I look around.

A little girl, three or four perhaps, is staring at me doubtfully, moving from one foot to the other in an arrhythmic dance. Behind her, her mum, I assume, smiles tentatively. 'You alright, love?' she asks. 'Need anything?'

'No, it's fine. Fine.' I sound perhaps a bit too sure. 'Just felt a bit sick in there for a moment, needed some air.' As if to prove it, I take a deep breath, and try to ignore my trembling hands. 'I'll be fine.'

The woman looks doubtful, but nods, smiles at me again in a way that makes it clear that she's still unconvinced, and takes her daughter's hand. The girl hopscotches her way round the corner and out of sight. As soon as they're gone I fish around again in my bag and pull out the order of service and stare at it accusingly. Why couldn't it have warned me? The name's wrong.

The marriage of Ms. Chloe Denise Harrison and
Mr. James Wingfield.

Then, out of the dim recesses of memory, I recall Dave telling me that James's new girl had been married before. I join the dots – Chloe Denise Harrison was once Chloe Denise Evans, which is why Mrs. Evans was sitting across the aisle from me as the mother of the bride, and why, without warning, twenty years slid away, and I was suddenly eleven again, remembering the last time I'd seen Chloe, and Mrs. Evans, and terrified, terrifying Abigail, stumbling out of the woods on that hot August morning.

I don't know how long passes, but suddenly Dave is there next to me. He's angry, I can tell, but trying not to show it. I've missed the wedding – his only brother's wedding, he points out, in case I'm not sure how much it matters to him – and he wants me to come back with him to the reception at the hotel. I stare blankly, a frightened animal, and shake my head.

'I can't, Dave,' I say. 'I just can't. I can't see them again.'

'Who?' he asks. 'See who again? We only flew in from Toronto yesterday and until we got here the only people we've seen have been the staff at the hotel and the car hire firm.'

'Look, it's a long story, and now isn't the time. But Chloe, and her mum – I know them. Knew them, anyway. I can't see them again. Please. Tell everyone I'm ill. That I must have picked up some bug on the flight or something. I don't know. Anything. You go to the reception. Tell James I'm really, really sorry. I'll go back to our room. Don't worry about me – I'll text you if I need anything. I just need to be on my own.'

He's grudging, but in the end he accepts it.

'Well, OK, but don't think you're out of the woods on this one, honey.'

I smile, in a way that makes it obvious that I'm anything but cheery.

'Oh, Dave, if you knew. If only you knew. I don't think I'll ever be out of the woods on this one. Not ever.'

He frowns, shrugs and turns away, tight lipped. 'I'll see you later,' he says.

*

Six hours pass. Some of it, probably, I'm asleep – at least, time passes in a hazy blur that I can't really remember. But some of it I spend on Facebook, searching via James's details to get to Chloe's, and then to her mother's. Mrs. Evans is clearly not a regular on Facebook, and posts very little, though there's an annual message and photo montage in tribute to 'our beautiful little girl'. It takes a while for me to realise that this is a reference to Abigail, and that she must have died, if my maths is right, eighteen years ago. Two years after, I think. There is no clue as to how she might have died, though my racing mind can spawn any number of theories.

Chloe's page is odd – well, not odd exactly, in that its subject matter isn't remotely out of the ordinary, but odd in terms of grammar. She writes about herself in first person plural, all the time, whether she's describing events she's recording as part of a group or just on her own. Some of it just about makes sense. There's a photo of her fingernails captioned 'Just had our hands done for our wedding', and I think maybe it's a simple error, where the first 'our' has been influenced by the fact that she was about to write the second one. But an earlier post has a picture of a fancy meal at some obviously busy restaurant, and she's written 'We really enjoyed our birthday lunch'. And so it goes on – a photo of Chloe and Mrs. Evans, with 'Mum takes us on holiday' below it; a shot of Chloe in front of a rail of dresses, labelled 'What are we going to buy next?' I'm puzzled, troubled.

Dave comes in about 9pm. He's obviously drunk quite a bit at the reception, but rather than collapse on the bed he's keen to talk. Some of it is just idle chat, about who said what at the reception, about the speeches and the toasts. He tells me that nobody really missed me once the meal was over, and even before then only because there was a gap in the seating plan at the top table.

Then he says, 'But it was funny at the wedding, though. Chloe kept nearly getting her lines wrong. You know, "Will you take this man…" and all that. She said, "We will – erm, that is, I will," and every time it came up she seemed to hesitate before saying "I" at all. You could hear a kind of rustling laugh in the congregation, especially from all her friends.'

'I know,' I say. 'It's the same on her Facebook page too. It's so weird.'

'I talked to James after the meal was over,' he says. 'I wanted to give him the chance to tell me all about her. He loves her lots, obviously. He's really protective of her. He said she'd had a tough life, with a family tragedy in her past.

Apparently she had an older sister, Abi I think she was called, who died in mysterious circumstances when Chloe was little, and it seems to have hit her hard. James reckons that all this stuff where she says "we" instead of "I" is because she's kind of carrying round the memory of her sister all the time. It's like she was responsible for it, or something.'

Inside, I can feel the waters rising again, but I press on. There's so much Dave and I haven't talked about, even though we've been together for nearly five years now, and it seems as good a time as any.

'Dave,' I say. 'This is hard for me – alright? Please be patient. There's lots of stuff about Chloe and her family I don't know – I don't know how or why Abigail died, for instance. But I have met Chloe before. Not for twenty years, but we were best friends back then. And you know about my panic attacks? Well, that's when they all started. Pour me a drink – there must be a little bottle of scotch in the minibar – and I'll tell you about it.'

He sorts out the drinks and we sit together on the bed. He holds my hand in his. Sometimes I shiver uncontrollably, sometimes it feels like minutes before I can continue, resting my head on my knees until the trembling subsides, but I get the story out. For the first time. For the first time ever. I've hidden this away from everyone, ever since. It feels like it's going to be a long night.

*

When I was eleven lots of things happened, some of them that only made sense to me years later. I know now that Mum and Dad's marriage was breaking up, but back then it was sold to me that Daddy had a job abroad and that Mummy was going to live in London with Auntie Ella for a while. I don't think I was sad, mostly because what I'd wanted to happen for years was about to come true. Rather than my boring local secondary school, I was going to start boarding school, and I couldn't wait for the adventures from all the books I'd read to happen to me too. It didn't turn out like that, of course, but at eleven it felt like all my wishes being granted.

That last summer before we moved away I must have spent every day with Chloe, not discussing what was going to happen next, because I guess we didn't have the maturity to talk about it, and in any case the summer seemed to go on forever, hot and dry and sunny, like summer holidays are supposed to do in childhood. We'd spend every day in the woods, at first just beyond Chloe's back garden, in case we got scared, but gradually going further and further into the darkness and the tangled undergrowth. It was ancient woodland, pretty much untended as far as memory serves, and it seemed to go on for miles. Bogeyman Woods, we called them. Our games got more and more elaborate, imagined worlds out of the Brothers Grimm, stories we'd act out, or variations on tales we'd make up as we went along, peopled with friends from school, and parents and teachers, or characters off the telly. It could have been idyllic.

The adult world was always there, of course, but sometimes it pressed in close. Both our mums had issued stern warnings, about keeping away from big boys, about not getting into trouble, about watching out for strange men. But we couldn't play and be watchful, not all at the same time. I remember once I lost my glasses in the woods, and Mum was furious with me. I never told her how it happened. I was playing, on my own as far as I remember – at least, I have no memory of what Chloe was doing – and I was marshalling an army of ants, guiding them between stones and piles of leaves, blocking their route or diverting it. I was lost to the world, on my hands and knees in the dirt, nose almost pressed against the forest bed as I and the army of ants inched along.

Suddenly, unannounced, I came upon a pair of old, torn boots, and rising out of them some tattered tracksuit bottoms, and out of them the dirt-encrusted body of a man. A tramp, I guessed.

'What you up to?' he said, 'Playing?'

I nodded, pointing to the ant trail.

'Here,' he said, with a grey, gap-toothed smile. 'I got something you can play with.'

He held out a hand to me, to help me up. His other hand had slipped inside his tracksuit bottoms, reaching in to pull something out. For seconds I froze. Then I scrambled back and stood up. Even then, as I remember it, I recall being unfailingly polite.

'Sorry,' I said. 'Have to go now. Mum wants me.'

And I turned and ran, haphazardly, frantically, not turning round, and I didn't stop until I reached the gate at the end of Chloe's garden, and it was only then that I realized I no longer had my glasses or the cardigan Mum had insisted I take with me.

Mostly, though, Chloe and I were together. We made a kind of treasure map of the woods, gave names to different locations or objects we'd found. There were animal trails - stray sheep and the occasional deer, I suppose now, but we made out they were proof of lions, perhaps, or unicorns. There were hardly ever people, or evidence of them. Once we came across a clearing where people had obviously camped, and there were the remains of a fire, plastic bags full of empty bottles of drink and torn open cartons of food. We pretended we were shipwrecked, drained the dregs out of the wine bottles, even though we hated the taste, and then pretended we were drunk or poisoned and in need of magic herbs to cure ourselves again. Was Abigail with us that day? I don't know. She's not in my memories, but that doesn't mean anything.

Abigail was – how should I put this now I'm adult? – Abigail was a girl with learning difficulties. I don't recall any physical disability, but she lolloped about in an uncoordinated way and was always falling over in the woods and hurting herself. I don't think she was with us every day. I have a hazy sense that she went off in a minibus to some sort of special school on some days, so maybe she was only in our care for the odd weekday or at weekends. She was thirteen that summer, bigger than we were, with that odd lumpy quality to her anatomy that I suppose I'd recognize now as the onset of puberty, but back then I don't think I was even aware that she was two years ahead of us in the acquisition of breasts and widening hips. She was just Abigail – heavier, fatter, awkward.

I'd like to say we welcomed her into our play, but I know it'd be a lie. When she was with us it was like a drag on our imaginations. Mostly we just bossed her about, made her into our slave, or a prisoner we'd captured, or someone we had to rescue. I don't recall her objecting to any of this, though she did sulk a lot, and cried when we ran off and left her behind.

'Tell Mum on you,' she'd say.

It was about as aggressive as she got. But as the summer wore on, I know Chloe resented her more and more obviously.

'Fat cow,' she'd say, though she knew it made Abigail cry.

The games became more exploitative. She was the donkey, on hands and knees, that one of us rode on, while the other pushed her along. We climbed trees and spat down on her, because we knew she didn't have the coordination to climb up with us. I recall this with nothing but shame. It was as though Chloe and I egged each other on to further and further humiliations, just because we could.

On that last day Abigail had been particularly trying. It was some kind of game of tag, but Abigail wouldn't wait until we'd hidden before coming to find us. Then Chloe found a coil of old washing line that must have been left behind by someone who'd been camping out, and said that if Abigail wouldn't wait we'd tie her to a tree and then she'd have to count to ten lots of times before she could loosen the bonds and come after us. I'm sure neither of us knew how to tie knots properly, so we just looped the line round the tree a couple of times, round Abigail's wrists and ankles and then tied it off in a clumsy bow behind the tree itself. Even before we finished, Abigail was crying. Chloe got more and more vindictive.

'Retard. Just a retard. That's all you are. Everyone says so,' she snarled.

I should have stopped it. I should have untied her, said it was just a game, and then we could all have gone home. But I didn't. We made Abigail promise to count to ten out loud very slowly, and then we ran off, screaming and laughing, flushed with cruelty and power. Eventually we stopped running, found a hiding place and sat still. The afternoon wore on. We wondered about Abigail, about how soon we'd hear her crashing through the undergrowth towards us. We talked about lots of things that day, much of it, I'm deeply ashamed to say, about how much better life would be if Abigail were to be lost in the woods forever.

As the shadows lengthened and the woods started to cool we looked around, and later we shouted Abigail's name for a bit. There was nothing. We couldn't find our way back to the tree where she'd been, but we did find a path that we knew led back to Chloe's house. When we got there, Mrs. Evans asked after Abigail.

'Oh, she's just behind us,' said Chloe, waving an arm vaguely in the direction we'd come from.

I had a drink and some cake, and then I went home, where Mum was packing for the house move. I'd gone to bed when Mum came into my room and asked if I knew anything about Abigail. Mrs. Evans had been on the phone, hysterical.

'I don't know, Mum,' I said, as the waters started to rise inside me. 'We were just playing.'

The next morning there were police at Chloe's house, and straggly trails of neighbours looking concerned near the front gate. Mum and I went inside, where Chloe, who had obviously been crying, was talking to Mrs. Evans and two female police officers. Mrs. Evans looked at me accusingly.

'Where's Abigail?' she demanded. 'Why hasn't she come home?'

I looked from her to Chloe, then up to Mum.

'I don't know,' I said. 'We were just playing.'

It must have been only a few minutes later when clumps of volunteers had been formed into an amateurish search party, and were about to set off into the woods. We were standing in Chloe's back garden, helpless, when we saw it. There was a sound like the lowing of a wounded animal, and the undergrowth stirred. In my memory we were all paralysed, rooted to the spot, though that might just be shock. Abigail pushed through the last of the brambles and bracken, out of the woods and in through the garden gate. She was naked. She was scratched and bleeding, but I was transfixed by her lumpen body, the bloody knees, the scarred breasts, the shadow of hairs at her groin, and the wordless O of her mouth and the terrified blankness of her eyes. It was years before I saw a reproduction of Edvard Munch's *The Scream*, but I recognized instantly what I was seeing. She was making no sound other than the bovine moaning, but then the world crashed around in buffeting waves, and I heard a wild hysterical screaming that went on and on until Mum slapped me to make me stop, and held me tight.

*

'Dear God,' says Dave, as I sit still on the bed, knees hunched under my chin. He holds my hand, but I feel exhausted and numb, and I'm hardly aware of it. For what seem like many minutes we stay like that. Inside, the waters are stilled again, for now at least. Dave gets me another drink.

'And?' he says.

'There's nothing much more,' I say, blankly. 'Abigail went off to hospital to be checked over, but she wouldn't speak, wouldn't talk to anyone. Maybe she never spoke again. Chloe wouldn't come and visit me, or even come and say goodbye when we moved. The week after that awful day, we left for London, then I went off to boarding school, and we never went back. It's as though my first eleven years are somebody else's life. I guess Chloe feels responsible for Abigail, for what happened to her. That's why her Facebook page is full of all this "We did this" and "We did that".'

'And you?' Dave is looking at me, as though for the first time. 'What do you feel?'

'I feel numb,' I say. 'Every now and then things come out of the woods and confront me, like some dumb, helpless, accusatory animal, and the waters start rising inside me. Oh, I've got tricks, strategies to fight the feelings off, games I play with myself to get them under control. But you know what you said, back there in the churchyard this afternoon, that I shouldn't think I'm out of the woods on this one...'

And I stare at him, blankly, as the whisky's fire burns down into my chest and the waters subside once more.

Patience

It's Saturday morning, and a familiar domestic routine for the financially-secure retired: we sit in the conservatory, surrounded by newspapers and coffee and pastries. I read the business pages, Hazel the news and arts. Recently – maybe it's age – she's taken to scanning the obituaries. There's a sudden intake of breath.

'John,' she says, hesitant, 'did you know about this?'

I take the paper from her, folded open at the obits, and even as I smooth it out in front of me, there's a constriction tightening at my throat. There's a photograph – an absurdly glamorous young woman with a cigarette dangling from her lip and wearing a Che Guevara beret, standing in front of a crowd in some public square. The writer's tone is polite but hints at the sardonic, as though the subject in question were not to be taken completely seriously. I make myself read.

'Heiress to the vast Stillman Pharmaceuticals empire, and variously a society beauty, a radical activist and, from time to time, a guest detained at Her Majesty's pleasure, Patience Stillman has died at the age of fifty-two, after a short illness. A riposte to nominative determinists everywhere, she was rarely patient and never still, espousing many of the fashionable causes of the late twentieth and early twenty-first centuries during her exceptionally vivid public and private career.'

I stop there, mostly because the print is becoming unaccountably blurry. Breathing and swallowing ought to be simple, reflex activities, but I have to concentrate to make them happen. I look up, stare out of the window into the space beyond the hedge at the bottom of the garden, my eyes focusing on nothing at all. I'm aware that Hazel is speaking.

'You all right? Thought you might want to read it, that's all. I'd lost track of Patience completely, I'm afraid. Selfish cow. Reading that, it looks as though she just went on picking people up and putting them down again to suit herself for the last thirty years. A trail of human wreckage, you might say.'

She notices that I'm barely responding.

'John, come on. Don't be so stupid. She screwed you over, like she did with everybody else. She made you pretty much unemployable, at least in the City. If Daddy hadn't had patience with you, I don't know where we'd be.'

She sighs, stands up, and takes the plates and cups off into the kitchen. I watch her retreating back, take one more deep breath, and feel I can trust myself to read on. The first skim, selfishly, is to reassure myself, but I appear not to have been mentioned directly. The writer comments fleetingly on 'her varied and complex personal entanglements', but names no names. The second read through, slower this time, fills out the story arc of Patience's life in the decades since she and I shared our last bewildered look across the court room.

Inside, I'm falling through empty space. The events are as present to me as if they'd been reported on today's news pages, not re-hashed for posterity in an obituary column. So, what is the most real thing, the bricks and mortar of our retirement villa that rewarded me for three tedious decades in financial management, or the three months, for that was all it was, when Patience Stillman directed the full glare of her shimmering sunlight straight into my dazzled eyes?

'Don't just stand there – come over here and hold this!'

I can see her now, as clear as if she were standing just the other side of the conservatory window. I hadn't actually planned to be on the Poll Tax demo. I was just walking down Oxford Street that Saturday afternoon when it sort of engulfed me, and I found myself jostled along by the increasingly vocal mob. That's when Patience, holding one end of a banner inviting Mrs. Thatcher to insert her poll tax somewhere uncomfortable, shouted across to me to grab the pole attached to the other end to keep it aloft. I often wonder what would have happened if I'd turned away and taken refuge in HMV, but I didn't – or couldn't. I'm no theologian or moral philosopher, so I'm not going to sit here debating free will with anyone, but it seemed to me at the time that all agency were taken from me, that I was there and with her and absorbed into her orbit in a heartbeat.

The march meandered on, then there was a sort of fragmentation, and it broke up into shards that splintered in all directions. We were aware of police on horses and wielding batons, of shop windows smashed and people running, falling, being dragged to safety, of blood and anger. Eventually the tide deposited us in a shop doorway, where I relaxed my grip on the banner and took stock. She was laughing at the chaos, dazzled and dazzling, murmuring, 'Brilliant – just brilliant,' to herself as if watching a particularly vivid bit of street theatre. At last she turned to me.

'That was awesome. Thanks. Thanks so much. You were great.'

Her smile held me. I must have seemed some kind of half-wit, grinning back at her. It was just like all the crappiest movie clichés you've seen – everything in slow motion, background sounds reduced to a muffled white noise, my heart thudding deafeningly in my ears, and her. I don't know how long we held that tableau, but then she laughed again, tossed her inevitably silky mane, and held out her hand.

'Immy,' she said.

'John,' I said. 'John.' It was as though I needed to say it twice, just to reassure myself of its reality.

'Well, my friends call me Immy. My name's Patience, but everybody says I should have been called Impatience, and that got shortened to Immy. Come on. Let's get a drink.'

And that's how it started. I could have said something innocuous – 'Thanks very much, but I've got to meet my family for dinner in a couple of hours,' or something like that – but I didn't. We went to a pub, had a few drinks, then a few more. She was garrulous, impassioned, angry with what she called bourgeois capitalism and the Tory bigots who rigged its systems, but angry in a way that made it all seem like the most outrageously glorious performance. She told me what she was going to do next, the meetings she would call, the speeches she would make, the groups she would contact, as though she were the director of this theatre, and would spare no expense to summon a cast of hundreds.

She was very – well, she was what my mother used to call 'very physical'. A few years later, after the death of Princess Diana and when the country was gripped in that odd mania of self-torturing grief, there would be lots of talk about how the nation was becoming more expressive, more emotional, more open to articulate its deeper feelings. Immy – Patience – was like that already. She touched me all the time – stroked my arm, held my hand in hers as she talked on, gripped me by the shoulder. I was lost. Helplessly, hopelessly, happily lost. At the age of 28, I was an adult in the sense that I had a job in investments, where I knew, thanks to the reforms of the Prime Minister whose status I'd recently been insulting, that lots of money was to be made. But emotionally, I think now, I was just some nervous beginner, barely able to swim and terrified of not being able to touch the bottom, and suddenly adrift in a raging torrent. I clung on to Immy. It was all I could do.

I didn't get home for two days, and then only to shave and change my shirt before arriving late to work. The interim was like living in a different dimension – a meeting in a squat where Immy introduced me as her boyfriend, a party in a warehouse that seemed to have been converted into an alternative performance space, overnight in Immy's flat, where I realised that my previous sex life had been like a perfunctory rehearsal for the real thing, and then the next day we were off down to Hampshire to help setting up some kind of camp in woodland off the A3 just before the bulldozers were due to move in.

I was dizzy, and not just from lack of sleep. This wasn't my world – the world of sensible shoes and sensible jobs and sensible pension provisions – and I suppose, looking back, I was like a kid on a roller-coaster ride. At the time, though, what I felt most strongly was that I was suddenly, intoxicatingly alive. The old world didn't let go its grip – at home my mother worried about me, at work Hazel's father took me into his office on more than one occasion for what he called 'a quiet word' – but it surely wasn't the real world after all. That was to be found strapped in the upper branches of a tree as the authorities closed in with their chain saws, or ferrying paint and placards and smoke flares to the next demonstration, or loved up on Es at a rave in a wood far down a rutted track in the wastes of rural Essex.

How long did all this last, I wonder? Ten weeks, twelve maybe. Immy was there almost all the time. She had the occasional trip to the continent – 'Just making contacts,' she'd say, or 'getting supplies' – but I'd meet her at Heathrow or Dover and we'd pick up from where we left off. The last Monday we were together started just like that. I'd taken the day off work, again, taken the train down to the coast and met her as she rolled off the ferry, and we drove back towards London, barely able to keep our hands off each other. I knew she had a meeting in Bath that evening, so I dropped her off at Paddington and drove back towards her flat in the City.

When the police stopped the car I thought nothing of it, except that I'd maybe been speeding, but when they started taking the door panels off and looking under the spare wheel compartment in the boot, I knew this wasn't a minor infringement. At the police station I kept expecting Immy to breeze in and explain that it had all been some simple mistake, but after I'd been charged there was nowhere to go except home and to take cover from the tabloid hacks, who were salivating outside my mother's house with sharpened pencils and a hunger for every sleazy detail. It felt like I'd been mainlining Immy and then suddenly left to face a come down with no support, and there was a week of such blank despair that even now it's simply a void. Mum fed me and tried not to talk about anything. Hazel called round – kind, dull, dutiful Hazel – with a message from her father. I was temporarily suspended from my duties, pending the outcome of the trial, but Hazel wanted me to know that she was working on her father to keep the door open for me when it was all over.

The trial, when it came, coincided with one of those odd periods of moral hysteria which infects the British justice system, the authorities and the media from time to time. Immy was the lightning rod of course – a child of the establishment who had turned her back on all that privilege, sexy and provocative in ways that pushed every tabloid button – but the drugs rap, which I was expecting, and the charge for owning an unlicensed shiny silver handgun, which I wasn't, spilled out from her to everyone of her acquaintance. It felt as though the Met wanted to use the case to hoover up every petty anarchist in the south-east of England. I pleaded ignorance, of course, but it's not the same as innocence, and I got six months for handling illegal goods and conspiracy to supply. Prison was a shock, naturally, but in the end it was no worse than the public school life of my teenage years, just with a different sort of bullying.

When I came out, Hazel was there, inevitably. I don't know what she saw in me. Perhaps I was a project for her – someone to save and get back on the rails – but she stood by me in the months that followed, and gradually it became known that we were 'seeing each other', in that rather anodyne phrase, and that Daddy had been encouraged to forgive me and, as long as I was always suitably chastened and grateful, and knew that I could never step out of line again, to take me back on board. The following year we were engaged and the year after that – how slowly time passed in the world of establishment approval – we were married.

There were strings attached, predictably. The most significant was that Immy – or rather, Patience, as she was now to be identified – was never to be mentioned again, on pain of who knows what horror. When she came out of prison there was unsurprisingly another tabloid flurry, but she sensibly took herself off abroad, and over the following decades there was only the occasional sighting in the press, as her activism took on a more environmentalist tinge – protesting against Shell in Nigeria, sitting in with South African gold miners, leading protests in the Amazon against tree-felling. I almost forgot what it felt like to be with her. Occasionally, in dull moments at work, I'd idly scroll through an online search to see where she'd gone next, but often whole years went by without so much as a twinge of yearning for those times to return.

And here I am. Retired in my late fifties, comfortably off, a pillar of the establishment, you might say. I play golf, keep an eye on my investments, patiently accompany my wife on foreign holidays, make dutiful noises at the bar of the local Conservative club. But today, with the newspaper still lying open on my lap, I wonder what it's all for. According to the obituary, Patience has been dead now for three days. As for me, I've been dead for the best part of three decades.

Interludes

I make a mental note: next time I'll travel first class, or go down the day before and squeeze the money out of the exam board for a night in a hotel. So much for a restful interlude before the Chief Examiners' meeting today. I scan the train carriage, packed to the gills, and can just make out a space at the far end, where my reserved ticket waves its middle finger at me. As I get closer my heart sinks. A mother and two small kids occupy three of the four places round the table. That's all I need – to be kicked on the shins by some whining brat all the way to St. Pancras. I put my document case down on the table, where the kid in the seat next to mine has spread his crayons, and say to the mother, as a warning to keep order, 'Excuse me, I think this is my seat.'

She looks up, flinches – yes, literally flinches – and then a blush starts deep at her neck, working its way across her cheeks. Still, who am I to talk? My ears burn. Surprise? Embarrassment? Memory? We've met before in, shall we say, rather different circumstances.

'Jenny?' There seems no need for the note of uncertainty. It is, without doubt, Jenny Carter, fifteen years older, maybe, and filled out a little with motherhood, but Jenny nevertheless.

'Mr. D,' she smiles. 'Or should I call you David, now we're both grown up?'

We shake hands – how terribly formal – and I settle into my place, pushing the crayoning book of the kid next to me gently across the table, opening my case and putting the exam board briefing papers on top of it. This ought to be a working trip. But I can't not acknowledge this surprising coincidence, not after … well, not after what happened.

'It's lovely to see you,' I say, and mean it. 'You're looking really well.'

'You too,' she says, though I know I've not aged quite so gracefully in the intervening years. 'Let you out for good behaviour,' she asks, 'or are you still on the exam marking treadmill?'

'Mr. Chief Examiner these days, I'll have you know. Risen through the ranks to this position of immense power, and, yes, the money's still crap, but somehow it impresses the parents, and God knows you need as much of that as you can get these days.'

She smiles, and, once the small talk is done – do you see anyone else from the old days, has that dragon of a Deputy Principal finally retired, and so on – we settle into an uneasy silence. Truth is, I don't know what to say. What do you say to someone you haven't seen for fifteen years, but who you last said goodbye to after clumsy and hasty but nonetheless urgent copulation in your personal office? Regret, and something like shame, stabs at me. The papers are full of sex and the abuse of power, whether Hollywood, Westminster or most places else. I feel I have to make redress, somehow. I move my papers around, knowing she'll look up from her phone, and hope for the best.

'Jenny, about the last time we saw each other.' She looks momentarily blank, and then she realises what I'm saying. 'I shouldn't have … that is, I-I should have done something, so that I didn't, we didn't…'

'What? Have sex on the floor behind the desk in your office?'

My turn to flinch now, and my ears burn again. I glance round, wondering what the woman across the aisle has heard, but she's staring stolidly at her laptop screen, the guy next to her is reading a book with his earphones in, the two kids at our table are absorbed in what looks like a toy version of a mobile phone or drawing. Maybe nobody has heard.

'Yes. That. I don't know what to say. I'm just really really sorry. I didn't mean to...'

'Bollocks!' she says. 'Nothing to apologise for. It wasn't you. It was me. It was that crazy interlude between A-levels and going to uni. I did lots of things that summer that I know I wouldn't do now – sorry, no offence – but I don't regret it.' She too seems aware of what's been in the news. 'Don't worry. I'm not about to have a #MeToo moment.'

I must look relieved, because she smiles across at me, suddenly eighteen again.

'Besides, I fancied the arse off you.'

Momentarily I wonder what an appropriate response to this might be, decide that engaging in intimate congress with an only just ex-student in a glorified stock cupboard has probably transgressed any professional codes that might apply, and settle on honesty.

'Mutual,' I grin.

'No, really,' she insists. 'We all did. What was it you called us in that class? The Sociology Feministas? You probably think we spent time over lunch in the canteen putting patriarchy in its place, but really we were discussing what we'd like to do with you if we ever got you alone in that office of yours at the back of the classroom. So, when I came into college on that day, I made really sure there was nobody else around, and that's just what I did. And anyway, you wanted it just as much as I did, I could tell. You were lonely back then.'

This cuts a little close to the bone, but she's right. Though I'd said nothing about my separation in college, students, especially the more attuned female A-level students, have a kind of sixth sense I guess. Then she glances down at my left hand, and the gold band on my ring finger.

'Happier these days?'

As soon as she's said it, she realises the mistake. Happiness is relative. My new marriage has done some things to ease the pain, but it's like bandaging a wound that will never heal. I confront, not for the first time today, or any day, the loss of Richard. You can imagine what it's like to lose someone, but the death of your own child is a grief like no other, a violation of nature. Even though it's nearly four years ago now, it's raw still.

'Sorry,' she says, her turn to apologise. 'I didn't mean to...'

'It's OK,' I try to reassure her. 'I'm learning how to manage. I can't do all that trite stuff about time being a healer yet, but I can talk without weeping. It's four years this August, after all.'

'I know,' she says. 'I was – that is, we were there. At the funeral, I mean. I don't expect you to have noticed. You were lost in your own pain. It was understandable.'

'We?'

'Me, and my kid sister.'

She's a bit uncertain now, I feel, though I suppose it's because she doesn't want the memory to hurt.

'You remember I have a younger sister? We used to talk about it a bit, at the slack times at the ends of lessons, because she and Richard were the same age. You know, what do you do to entertain an eight-year-old?'

These memories are much hazier, but I can dig down to them. The small talk – 'have a good weekend?' – and Jenny saying she'd babysat for her sister (Alice, was it?) and run out of videos to watch, and anyway what can you do when you can't have a proper conversation with a small child. It had the stab of truth about it, I recognised, from times when I'd had Richard for the weekend and we were both bored by Saturday lunchtime.

'I remember now,' I nod. 'But still, why were you at the funeral?'

'She was there. Alice, that is. She was with Richard, when it all happened, I mean. Sorry. I don't mean to remind you. But there were twelve of them, after their A-levels, out in Ayia Napa, just letting off steam. Alice was in that group.'

It feels like there's something she's not saying, here, but I'm guessing she's just being careful with my memories.

'Ah.' The truth is, this surprises me a bit. I force myself to confront the past. At the time I'd barely seen Richard for a few years. When he was twelve he decided to side with his mum and mostly stopped coming to see me. When Ellen rang out of the blue, and just wailed, 'My baby's gone,' it took a long time before what she said made any sense, and when it did I just kind of shut down. Eventually I discovered he'd been stabbed outside a nightclub in Ayia Napa, but after that I didn't want to know anything else, didn't want to feed my imagination any more.

And now this is odd. I get out my phone, sort through the photographs, and show them to her. Richard as a toddler, on the junior school football team, and things I'd had posted to me since, Richard learning to drive, standing with his A-level results slips, thumbs up to the camera. That would have been just before. Yes, just before.

She finds them more moving than I'd expected. Then the child on her side of the table wants to see, so he looks, without interest. Then, as she's passing the phone back, so does the kid next to me, who's spent what feels like the past hour burrowing into my ribs.

'No, Ricky. Give the gentleman his phone back.'

'It's all right,' I say, and show the pictures to him.

He's solemn, thoughtful even.

'This is my little boy,' I say, 'though he was quite a big boy in the end. Taller than me, anyway. Look here.'

I swipe across to the image of Richard as a toddler.

'He must have been about your age when I took this. See, he's got lovely golden curls, just like you.'

Eventually, I get my phone back, and we all drift a little, Jenny texting urgently, the kid opposite me playing with his toy phone, the one next to me drawing intently. I pick up and try to lose myself in my papers. Then, from opposite, 'Mummy, I want a wee.'

'We're nearly there, Sam. Can't it wait?'

It's obvious that it can't, so Jenny takes Sam's hand.

'You coming, Ricky?' she asks, but the boy next to me shakes his head, gravely. She looks across at me, evidently sorry for landing me with impromptu child care, but I shrug and nod at her.

'It's fine,' I say, and they head off down the carriage.

While they're gone, Ricky shows me his indecipherable drawings – this is him with his mummy, this is him playing with Sam – and he looks up at me in a way that's oddly familiar, almost trusting. Then Jenny and Sam are back, noisy and bustling, and the stillness is broken. When everyone is settled, I offer sympathy.

'You must have your hands full, bringing up twins.'

She smiles. 'Not twins. Sammy here is mine, and Ricky is my sister's. I've just been looking after him for a few days to give her a break while she finishes her dissertation. We're so proud of her, completing her degree and postgraduate work and bringing up her baby too.'

'That's very unusual these days,' I say, hoping to sound impressed. I do a quick mental calculation, decide Alice must be twenty-two at the most, and know I can't raise the issue of why she had a child and not an abortion if she found she was pregnant at eighteen.

Jenny is as intuitive as ever.

'She was very young, but from the start she was determined to have the baby. It turns out she got pregnant around the time she was on holiday in Ayia Napa. I think it helped that I was pregnant too, so we went through lots of things together. Sam and Ricky are two weeks apart.'

'The father...?'

'Ricky's dad isn't around any more.'

There's an awkward silence. In my mind I can't help but see a drunken one night stand, barely a memory of the event and not even knowledge of the father's name. But I can't say it, obviously.

Then suddenly, here we are. The train grinds to a halt, we bustle about making sure that the children's clutter is all bagged up, and I help them down onto the platform. She's off to greet her sister. I have my meeting. We say goodbye. I give Jenny a hug, tousle Sam's hair, and shake Ricky gravely by the hand.

Then all this happens as if in slow motion. I step onto the escalator that will take me down to the tube line. As we're parting I hear Ricky ask, 'Auntie Jenny, who was that man?'

Jenny's reply is brisk. 'He used to teach me at big school.'

'Will we see him again?'

And, as they're moving out of earshot, faintly, behind the intrusive urgency of the tannoy, she says, 'Well, that really depends on your mummy.'

I stagger a little. It's like a blow to the stomach, knocking the wind out of me. I turn, but behind me on the left of the escalator is a long phalanx of commuters, staring fixedly ahead. On the right, an army marching ever downwards. I try to fight back up against the tide, but it's futile, and the mechanism carries me slowly, inexorably down and away from where I want to be. I push into the right-hand line, walk down the escalator, cursing its idiot slowness, race around to the up side, and work my way frantically back to the level I was on before. There is no sign of them. Everywhere there are people milling, glassy-eyed, in that dead zombie bustle of London. I clutch my document case to my chest, staring, breathing, lost.

Eventually I sit down, gripping my case to me as my heart stops racing. It's one of those moments when I know without being told. No wonder she flinched when she saw me. Not some post-A level sexual indiscretion. No wonder she was uneasy when I showed Ricky my photos. Not the worry about his sticky fingers on my phone. No wonder she was cryptic about Alice. Not the shame of teenage motherhood.

My grandson.

The Missing Pages

She scrolls through the messages on her mobile. Nothing new from him, nothing since the last one: 'See you under the clock once you've got through the barrier.' The train slows as it navigates the final approach to the station. The lump in her throat gets harder to ignore. She's spent the last two hours telling herself she's not scared but now the moment has arrived she can't stop her hands shaking. What if he doesn't like her? And underneath that, what if he isn't like he says he is? To distract herself she checks again through her shoulder bag. A couple of changes of clothes. Hairbrush and toiletries. Phone charger. Bank card and some cash in a pink fluffy zip-up purse. A showerproof jacket she put in at the last minute when she realised it might be raining in London. And the torn-out pages from the photo album.

The train slows to a stop and she watches the others in the carriage standing up, checking their belongings and filing down the aisle to the exit doors. Her legs feel weak, but she forces herself to stand up too. She has wanted this moment to arrive for weeks, but now that it has she feels so alone, so unprepared for what might happen. She sees one of the train staff with a big bin liner working his way down the carriage collecting empty plastic cartons and drinks bottles and stray magazines. She could tell him she got the wrong train by mistake, that she needs to go back to Sheffield to her mum and dad and big sister. She could tell him she's about to meet a man she's never actually seen before in real life and now she doesn't think she wants to.

Except that she does. She checks her reflection in the carriage window. Time to go.

*

'God, it's so boring.' She looks at Janine for some acknowledgement of the utter tedium of a fifteen-year-old's life. 'Nothing ever happens. School. Home. School again. Home again. Tea. Homework. Telly. Bed. School again.'

She throws a bit of screwed-up paper at Janine's head, and checks her phone. Nothing.

'Well,' says Janine, sixteen and so infinitely closer to the currently unattainable excitement of adulthood. 'Your folks are, well, a bit weird. So old. Nobody's mam and dad should be that old.'

She throws the paper back at Megan and laughs.

'Do you ever, you know, try to imagine them,' says Janine, 'you know, getting it on.'

'Ewww.' Megan pulls a puke face. 'That's gross.'

'Well,' says Janine with the wisdom of age, 'they must have got you somehow.'

*

That night in bed Megan has what she will later think of as an out-of-body experience. She's still in bed, obviously – she knows there's a row of stuffed toys on the shelf by her bed, beneath the poster of the boyband she ought to have taken down two years ago – but at the same time she's looking down at everything from a great height, watching everyone in the house. She can see through the walls and floors and everything. Mother and Father, side by side in the living room watching *News at Ten*, and moments later side by side in their twin beds under those old-fashioned matching bedspreads, just their tiny heads sticking out from under the covers. On Mother's bedside table are the fading bouquet and the card that says 'Happy 60th'. Father is even older. He'll be 65 next month. She's never known a time when they weren't old.

Janine's right. Nobody's mam and dad should be that old. All her friends – no, this is an occasion for being honest with herself – both her friends have parents who are young, who go running and to aerobics classes and have at least heard of the people who make the music she and Janine listen to. Mother and Father want her to be tidy and responsible and punctual and to eat up all her greens and be grateful. On the rare occasions Megan asks them if she can do anything, Mother will purse her lips and say, 'Oh, I don't think so, do you, Father?' and Father will look up and over his paper and say, 'Whatever Mother says, dear.'

But from her vantage point overlooking her quiet street with her X-ray vision, Megan can see through the rest of the house, into the back bedroom where Sophie, her big sister, is half reading a book in the gloomy pool of her bedside light, listening with half an ear to the radio, counting down the minutes till she ought to get some rest before tomorrow's presentation at work and wondering – Megan realises this with a start; she hadn't expected the X-rays to see into people's minds too – what has become of her life.

There has barely been a moment when Sophie has not been there. There are hardly any family photos anywhere on the walls, but Megan loves the one on the landing at the top of the stairs: Sophie on the seafront somewhere sunny with the light sparkling off the water and grinning at the camera, pushing a buggy containing a contented Megan in a floppy sunhat and candy-stripe dungarees. It's only now, with her X-ray insight, that Megan wonders who took the shot. Mother and Father don't seem to be there. But who else could it have been? As she grew up, Sophie was always the one to take Megan to the park or the swimming baths. She went with her to dancing lessons and horse riding. She went to Megan's primary school play. Father was always at work – 'Your Father's so busy just now and he won't be able to come' – and Mother seemingly had to stay at home, to make sure the dinner was ready.

Out-of-body Megan has a moment of vertiginous queasiness. Looking down into Sophie's room, now she can see Sophie scrolling through her phone messages. She looks closer. Sophie wipes her eyes with the back of her hand, tosses the phone aside, searches at the back of her wardrobe and pulls out a hard-back book and turns the stiff leaves one by one. Megan feels she ought not to look, but can't stop herself. Sophie finds the place midway through the album, seizes a couple of pages by the corner and tears the laminated sheets out with a brutal finality. Megan watches as she stuffs the excised pages in a drawer, pushes the photo album back in the wardrobe and puts out the light as she gets back into bed. Megan knows she ought not to be able to see in the dark, but she knows Sophie is weeping. It is a moment of revelation. Sophie is thirty-one years old, and weeping in her childhood bedroom. Megan feels there are no words for this, but as she returns to her physical body and looks up for reassurance to her shelf of stuffed toys she discovers an empathy unusual in a fifteen-year-old. Life is not just boring. It is full of grief.

*

Dishonesty does not come easily. Megan has indulged in no meaningful sins of commission, as she will later come to know them. She is not even aware of sins of omission at fifteen, at least not beyond a general feeling of guilt and embarrassment as she walks past the man with the stray dog on a piece of string outside the shopping centre and knows it would be better if she gave him something but doesn't think he'll want any of her backpack of school books. Conformity has been stamped onto her consciousness over the years: never misses school unless she's really really sick, always hands in homework on time, tidies her room well before the need to read any kind of riot act.

Probably searching through Sophie's wardrobe makes her feel more guilty than anything else in her life. Certainly guiltier than watching that porn film in Janine's bedroom last summer, even if it stirred something inside her that she hadn't known was there until then. But when she gets home from school the day after her nocturnal experience, she waits until Mother is busy in the kitchen – both Father and Sophie are still out at work – and tries not to disturb anything in her search for the album. She's about to give up when she feels the ridges of its spine. She perches awkwardly on the edge of Sophie's bed and turns the leaves in wonder.

Sophie's life is laid out in images she's never seen before. A toddler holding the hand of a strange woman who turns out on closer inspection to be a much younger version of Mother. A four-year-old with a face covered in ice cream. What looks like a school trip to Castleton – Megan recognises the entrance to Speedwell Cavern. There are school friends and pictures of a hockey team, part of a past that might have come from another age. Megan is tempted to laugh at the hairstyles and the funny, high-waisted trousers, but with her new-found realisation of her sister's plight the emotional and physical distance from that world seems terribly poignant.

The last images before some pages have been torn out seem to come from a foreign holiday. There are shop fronts with what looks like French on the advertising hoardings. Megan finds this very strange. Mother and Father never go on holiday – Father's days off work are spent on the allotment and Mother, well, Mother has never mentioned going on holiday, ever. Sophie and a group of friends – all about Megan's own age – wear berets and have drawn moustaches on their upper lips with what looks like felt tip, and it looks as though they haven't been able to take the shot without someone in the group collapsing in hysterics. The innocence grips Megan by the throat.

After the torn-out pages the tone of the album changes. There are still some shots of Sophie on her own – a gaunt face staring back at the camera from what looks like Alton Towers – but in most of the snaps what strikes Megan most is her own presence. These are more images like the one at the top of the stairs. Sophie must have taken care of her almost from the word go. Was Mother ill after I was born, wonders Megan. After a few more pages the pictures peter out. Perhaps Sophie lost interest in keeping a photo album. Perhaps cameras on mobiles just got so much better and now all Sophie's snapshots are saved digitally.

Suddenly the sound of a key in the front door snaps Megan back into the present, and there is just time to stuff the album back into place, push the door to Sophie's bedroom shut and throw herself down on her own bed with a random schoolbook before there are footsteps on the stairs and Sophie appears to ask her how her day's been.

Finding the torn-out pages takes longer and feels more guilty-making still. In a simpler world Megan would just ask her sister about her life, satisfying a curiosity she's never felt until now. But if Megan is learning anything, it is that life is not simple. She feels bound to be caught in the act, sifting her way through Sophie's bedroom without leaving a trace, and at one point feels guilty enough to want to give up. Maybe Sophie has destroyed everything. Then, under the lining paper at the bottom of a drawer of old jumpers, Megan feels the shape of the missing pages.

In the days that follow she can barely meet Sophie's gaze, expecting every conversation to lead to an accusation. For some time Megan simply smooths out the pages and turns them silently, but always there's the itch to know more. Once she peels off the laminated surface she knows there is no chance of getting the images back into Sophie's bedroom intact, but she has to know – who is this with Sophie and (Megan's heart misses a beat) who stares at the camera with Megan herself on his shoulders. The back of many of the pictures is blank, but a few contain a scrawled date, a location, a name. It is enough.

*

'How do you know he's for real?' Janine asks. 'You must have sat through those "Sex and Relationships" sessions in tutor group like I did. You know, never believe that someone on the internet is who they say they are.'

Megan blushes. 'It's not like that,' she says. 'He's – he's really nice. Look' – she gets out her mobile – 'he's sent me a photo.'

It was more complicated than that, but Janine doesn't need to know the details – how she put her profile on Facebook, figuring that's where he might look, and then waited, waited, until slowly the messages came.

Janine wants to shake her. 'You can't do it. You mustn't go. He'll be some fifty-year-old pervert who'll lock you in his house and rape you and then bury your body. He's probably jacking himself off every time he has a WhatsApp conversation with you. God, girl, you know nothing about life. Nothing.'

She grips Megan by the wrist, her voice freighted with experience.

'Listen, Megs. Just listen to me. Men are shit. They'll tell you anything. They're only after one thing. Look, I'll let you into a secret. Weekend before last I went round to Shane's, when his folks were away overnight. Said he fancied me and that he'd always done. So we did it. Afterwards it turns out he's changed his mind. Don't want that to happen to you, with some, like, some creep from London with a fake profile. Just don't. Please. Promise me.'

Megan looks at her. She's never seen Janine acting with such passion, such intensity.

'Alright,' she says, swallowing hard. 'I won't go. Not yet, anyway.'

She is shocked at herself. When did lying start to come so easily?

*

On the platform, she takes out her phone again. Still no more messages. Surprise mixed with fear. Surely he'd have texted her when the train came in. She scrolls back through the WhatsApp conversations of the past ten days, their hesitations, suggestions, promises, seeming truths. What if Janine is right? Her eye is snagged by a message from a week ago. 'Don't tell anyone at home. This is our secret for now.' She knows what Janine would make of that. Back at home, they'll know by now that she's gone, but not, she imagines, where. Sophie will have gone to work, but maybe Mother will ring her and let her know. Probably Mother or Father might contact Janine sometime soon to see if she's gone round there, and then what? She doesn't trust Janine to keep her mouth shut. Best get on with it.

She pushes through the gate and looks round at the expanse of the station, its crush of people scurrying past, the scale of the brick and glass taking her breath. On the far wall she makes out a huge ornamental clock face, and there he is. There's a moment's panic. He's so much older than the photo he sent, but then, she rationalises, he would be. He holds out his arms to greet her, but she stops, a few feet away, suddenly a child again.

'Megan?' he asks.

She nods, the lump back in her throat. She feels like a frightened animal, as though she's been caught in a trap. He offers to take her bag, but she shakes her head.

'Coffee?' he asks.

She pulls a face. Coffee is for grown-ups.

'Hot chocolate?' he suggests.

A smile. A nod.

'Here,' he says. 'This way.'

Seated by the window overlooking the concourse, he pushes the hot chocolate in her direction. She sips awkwardly. It's too hot, but she needs to do something, and conversation just won't come. Finally he pulls an envelope from his jacket pocket, spills out its contents onto the table before them and sorts the photos into groups. She reaches into her bag for the torn pages from the album.

The images stare back up at them both. For a moment the silence between them is full of emotion. He clears his throat, pressing at the corner of his eye with a fingertip.

'Does Mum know?' he asks.

She shakes her head. 'Not yet,' she says.

For more moments still they remain silent, staring down at the snapshots. A young woman and a young man. A child sitting on his shoulders. The weight of years presses down on both of them.

He clears his throat again. 'Another chocolate?' he asks.

She nods. 'Thanks, Dad,' she says.

Pancake Day

This is the story of Pancake Day. Though really, I realise, this is a story of shame, a story that would have lain buried, half-forgotten to my last breath, without the district nurse.

'Were your folks Cole Porter fans?' I ask, as she leans across me to finish cleaning the wound before she starts re-dressing it. She frowns, concentrating. I wait until she's finished setting the old dressing aside and ask again, nodding at the name badge at her lapel.

'Your mum and dad. They must have known, surely.'

And tentatively, barely a croak because much more than that feels like it might hurt too much, I start to croon. *'Night and day, you are the one. Only you beneath the moon, under the sun...'*

The effort is too great. I can feel the rumblings of a cough that I dearly don't want to rise to the surface.

She frowns again, disapproving. 'Mr. Nicholls,' she says, 'you know as well as I do the risks here. It's imperative that we keep this wound clean, so I need to concentrate on my job. You need not to put any strain on the stitches, so that means no coughing, no sneezing, and definitely' – a ghost of a smile – 'no singing.'

Minutes later and the job is done. She seems like briskness personified, but as she's tidying away the torn packaging from the dressings and bandages, she looks up.

'So, you were saying?'

'Your name badge,' I say. '"Tina Knighton-Day, District Nurse". Did your mum and dad hyphenate it or had it already happened?'

There's a pause. I can see her thoughts: don't have personal conversations with patients.

Then she says, 'It was my mums' idea.'

'What did your dad think?'

'No – my mums. Both of them. It was their idea.'

'Oh, I'm sorry,' I stumble, 'I – I didn't mean –'

'It's all right,' she says. 'It's a normal thing to assume. But they'd both brought me up since I was tiny, and so when the chance came for them to get married, they wanted to use both their names, and they'd been so good to me and my sister that we both changed our names too.'

A shadow flits across the curtain of my mind. A memory I didn't even know was there. I can't stop myself. I need to be sure. I try to sound casual, innocent.

'And were they nurses too, your mums?' I ask.

She shakes her head. 'No chance,' she says. 'No, they were in education, teachers, both of them. Well, my birth mum was, all her life. She's been retired ten years, thank goodness. My other mum was a bit different. She did all sorts. Teaching to start with – that's how they met – but she was an athlete, a runner, and she got into sports science and coaching and all that stuff. You might have heard of her. Nicola Day. She was on TV a lot about ten, fifteen years ago. The BBC's go-to person for programmes about fitness and exercise.'

I try to keep my face as blank as possible. I shrug, non-committal.

'Sorry – doesn't ring any bells.'

'Anyway, must be going,' she says, back in professional mode. 'You've got all the instructions' – she points to the leaflet, with its cheery pictures of post-op treatment for aortic aneurisms – 'what to do, what not to do. I'll be back the day after tomorrow to change the dressing again, and make sure the wound's healing cleanly. And remember,' she says, frowning over her glasses, 'no singing.'

She smiles. 'I'll see myself out.'

*

Adolescence in an all-boys grammar school south of Manchester in the 1970s was not the place to receive a balanced education, either academically or in life. A menagerie of teachers, many of them with hindsight obviously still scarred from wartime experiences, and an inchoate mass of teenage boys struggling with puberty trapped in an almost exclusively male environment weren't a good combination if one wanted to emerge into adulthood socially well-adjusted. At my age I tend to think I've come out of the experience quite well, though it took years for me to learn how to talk to a woman without expecting her to make either my tea or my bed.

It's the nicknames that give it away, that sense that other boys weren't actually people, but objects. When in the decades that followed they appeared in a totally different context, their nicknames came out of the past with them. Duncan Jarvis terrorised my form group for five years; when I saw one night on the news that he'd been sentenced for violent assault and threats to murder, I just thought, 'Ah, Psycho Jarvis – what else would you expect?'

I wonder now how my contemporaries felt, reduced to labels. Fatty Oates, obese and never allowed to forget it, or Griffiths, Griff the Whiff, surrounded by his own personal atmosphere of urine. And worst of all, those who dared to have a trace of a personality, or to stand out from the crowd. Fairy Robinson, whose voice didn't break until he was fifteen, and who always ended up playing female roles in school productions. Farting Garting, whose skills in some areas were famous, though you wouldn't want to be caught in the same room as him for long. And Wanker Evans... Well, you get the picture.

Teachers too. They carried their nicknames, some of them, like shields into battle. Cruncher Harris: one to avoid in the annual staff/student football match. Dead-Eye Davies: a perfect shot with a board rubber, though I wonder why he never ended up in court. Some of them had nicknames that were echoes of earlier days. Soapy Kirk, still called Soapy when I started secondary school even though Kirk's Soaps had been absent from the shelves of local shops for well over a decade. My French teacher in the sixth form, universally known as Scab, though even a trace of humanity would have shown us that the wrecked surface of his face and hands must have been a daily torture to him. And One-Ball Forbes, who ought to have been known as the best Latin teacher I ever had, but whose special burden in life was to have been rumoured to have once had testicular cancer.

So, an all-male, testosterone-fuelled, empathy-free zone. There were women, of course, but they were behind the hatch in the kitchens or, hair immaculately coiffed, typing earnestly in the office. There was a girls' convent school across the main road, so these mysterious, inaccessible creatures with their strangely curvy bodies and their baffling tendency to hug each other were there, peripherally, but never actually part of our lives.

*

I must have been fourteen, I think, when the school hired its first female teacher. Looking back, it was probably thought of as a progressive move on the part of the school management, an attempt to drag this emotionally repressed institution into the later 20th century. Back then, though, it just felt weird. What to call her? 'Miss,' she said, though we knew – Tony 'Orange' Peel lived just down the road from her – that she had two young daughters, Cassie and Christina; later, as a concession to her individuality, 'Miss Knighton'. A small, pear-shaped woman, trying to teach us Maths, whilst we struggled with the smell of perfume as she waddled down the rows of tortured souls, dispensing advice on how to balance equations. 'Miss Knighton', of course, would never do in the brutal world of schoolboy nicknames. After a while as Fat Arse (there were few prizes for originality), Psycho Jarvis nailed it. 'Look at her,' he said, as she padded the corridor, 'with her droopy tits.' And so: Droopy Tits Knighton, later DT Knighton, or 'DT' for short.

The year after, there were five more female members of staff. I remember we lost one of the boys' toilet areas to be turned into a female staff 'rest room'. There seemed to be a greater emphasis on minding our language on corridors and in the dining hall. But this is where it gets difficult. I was starting my O-levels, and English was beginning to be important to me – not just another subject but something that was starting to thaw the frozen emotions that had built up around my heart. On the first day of term I saw on my timetable that I had a new teacher, Dr. N Day. The 'Dr.' was a mystery in itself. Who would he be? The only 'Dr.' I knew was at the surgery, a portly man with nicotine-stained fingers and a heavy moustache who had told my mum I had to have my tonsils out.

When a tall woman in a man's suit with briskly tied-back hair placed her briefcase imposingly on the teacher's desk and looked us up and down, I felt – what? Confusion, certainly. Affronted, possibly. What could a woman know about books? But gradually, as the weeks passed, and she unfolded the quiet mysteries of the poetry of Thomas Hardy, daring us to experience tenderness and loss and regret, I think what I came to feel was, oddly, the validity of being able to feel at all, to recognise and name emotions after years of stuffing them down into my sports bag with my muddy football kit. I don't think I was to discover what love was for some considerable time, but this was a fifteen-year-old's equivalent. I'd begun my journey of discovery, Dr. Day as my guide.

Of course, all around me the brutality of the rest of the school ground on. Dr. Day too acquired an epithet. How could it be otherwise? What did we know about her? According to Tony Peel, she had moved into DT's house, where she had a room. He'd seen her talking to DT's kids as they waited at the bus stop, and later we'd all seen her folding herself into DT's battered old Mini at the end of the school day. None of that helped with a name.

But Psycho Jarvis had, for someone otherwise so Neanderthal, a gift for this sort of thing. Dr. Day was six foot of skin and bone, making no concessions to the anticipated curves of the female form, and entirely flat-chested. To Psycho it was obvious: Droopy Tits Knighton and Pancake Day, a double act to entertain the school. We knew it was right: we knew about Morecambe and Wise, Little and Large, we'd even seen films of Laurel and Hardy. It hurt my sense of her humanity a little, this woman who was opening up my world to the subtleties of feeling, but no matter. Pancake Day is what she became.

How do you measure the passage of time as an adolescent? Ball-achingly slowly and disappearing with terrifying speed, it seemed. Day after day of monotony, relieved by odd moments of shared pleasure. We learned about Offa's Dyke in Geography, and a couple of the more artistic ones tried to draw her on the inside cover of their books, an outcome leading to detention and dark mutterings about getting parents in; the rest of us settled for a communal snigger whenever the name was mentioned.

But what I know now, forty years later, is that Pancake Day was my solace and my inspiration. I began to talk about studying English at university to Mum and Dad. I asked her for more things to read, found Hardy's poetry led me to his novels, found they led me to George Eliot (too serious) and Dickens (too sentimental), but the poetry of Tennyson and particularly Matthew Arnold felt like it was written with a sixteen-year-old in mind, all imagined longing and desolation, full of love thwarted and lost. I began to find reasons to stay behind at the ends of lessons, to talk to her about what I thought, flattered by the attention, flattered that she seemed to find me a worthy person to talk to.

It stands to reason that all that would have got me marked as a swot, and a recipient of ritual beatings at the hands of Psycho and his lumpen sidekicks. Fortunately, I'd always been good at sport, and during that year I found that I could run – not fast, necessarily, but seemingly forever. Would it spoil my tale if I said that Pancake was my inspiration there too? She was a cross-country runner of some repute, we discovered. When she took over the moribund running club from Scarface Dixon in Metalwork, a surprising number of us dug out old running shoes and took to pounding the local parks and hillsides, always trailing along behind Pancake Day, with her oddly upright, high-stepping gait, long legs eating up the ground like some pedigree racehorse, but always sufficiently encouraged by her stern, mannish enthusiasm to turn up the following week. A couple of us showed enough promise for there to be talk of entering the regional championships. She talked to us about technique, about diet, about motivation. Run of the mill stuff now, of course, but then it felt like gaining access to arcane knowledge, a kind of initiation.

As that year came to an end I could no longer hide it from myself. I was in love with Pancake Day! I expected nothing back, of course, happy for it all to be unrequited and those visions of her lithe frame pounding across the playing field to be the subject merely of my late-night fantasies. But in the summer term I talked to her about studying English at A-level, about the best places to go to university, about – dizzying heights – Oxbridge entrance exams.

And then I broke the spell. I said at the start that this is a story of shame. Shame is a socially-generated emotion.

You can't feel it on your own. It has to be triggered by your relationships with others, an act of degradation that alters your standing in your own eyes because of how you relate to the rest of the world. It hurts to remember, even now. The weekend Dr. Day went off to run at the National Cross-Country Championships was one I paid particular attention to. I knew that amongst the moto-cross and horse-racing and darts on *Grandstand* that Saturday afternoon, the BBC cameras would be following both the men's and women's races. I made sure Mum wasn't going to want to watch the wrestling on ITV, and settled down to enjoy the action.

I had no doubt whatever that she would win. It was a given. If I'd been old enough or savvy enough to have laid a bet, I'd have put all my accumulated paper-round money on it. As the camera homed in on the leading runners covering the last half-mile, I felt a pleasure that was almost erotic in knowing that this was our Dr. Day, my very own Pancake, who strode out in front to take the tape. That's when it happened. Runners finished the race, slumping to their knees or standing, hands on hips, gasping for air. But Pancake strolled on, unruffled, to the fringes of the crowd and there – in the corner of the screen by now but, by God, on national TV – she and a small, dumpy woman engaged in a long and passionate embrace. Nowadays, of course, I could scroll back and watch that again, or at least see it repeatedly on iPlayer. There'd be dozens of uploaded clips on YouTube. Then, though, it was but a moment – and then it was gone. Except it wasn't. It was seared on my consciousness. Pancake, my Pancake, the subject of my naively unwholesome nocturnal visions, in mid-snog with Droopy Tits herself, regardless of who was watching.

I could have kept it to myself. I could have used it as a lesson in growing up, a first, chaste heartbreak to prepare me for far worse to come. But I didn't. On Monday morning I sought out Psycho Jarvis and told him what I'd seen. The blue touch paper having been suitably lit, I watched the action play out in all its inevitable and tawdry horror. Within days the knowledge was all round the school, crude and artless artworks in the corners of blackboards, innuendoed messages left in casually public places, gossip overheard and repeated, amplified until it seemed that everyone was in on the story. And my doing, all my doing. Of course, Dr. Day continued to encourage me, to encourage all of us, until the end of the summer term, before the long wait for results day and then the start of life in the sixth-form.

But it wasn't the same. It couldn't be. I had shattered an illusion, and paid for it with a guilt all the more anguished for being private. At the start of the new academic year, I was not surprised to find that neither Mrs. Knighton nor Dr. Day were on the staff any longer. I completed my A-levels, of course, even did an English degree with sufficient competence to follow it with a Ph.D. ('Love and Loss in the Verse of Minor Victorian Poets'), Dr. Nicholls no less. But through it all, I knew what I'd done, what wounds I'd opened that I didn't know would ever heal again.

*

When the district nurse arrives I know what I have to do. I've rehearsed the speech in my mind until I'm pretty much word perfect. I've searched the internet in the past couple of days; I know Dr. Nicola Day died two years ago, of breast cancer ironically, given her nickname of old, a great athlete in her time and a charismatic broadcaster of considerable promise, according to the obituary I'd read. I can't do anything for her now, but I can at least make suitable confession to the woman she helped to bring up. I bide my time, wait until the dressing has been changed – 'You've been doing as you're told, I see!' – and seize the moment.

'Before you go,' I say, 'can I talk to you for a moment?'

I must sound more solemn than usual because Ms. Knighton-Day looks up, puzzled.

'Of course,' she says, 'what is it?'

'I've got something to say to you,' I say, then wait for the lump in my throat to go away, 'something about your mothers, and their past.'

'Mr. Nicholls,' she says, 'what's wrong? Look, don't get upset. You don't want to get in a state, it'll be bad for you, for your, you know' – she gestures at my abdominal stitches.

'Sorry,' I try again, startled at the unaccountable trembling in my chest. 'Look, I don't know how to say this, except to say it. Your mums, when they were younger, they taught at the secondary school I went to, and I – well, I caused them to leave. It was my fault. I started a rumour and it, it cost them their jobs.'

'Mr. Nicholls,' she says, 'here. Here, don't take on so.'

She finds me a tissue, puts a hand on my arm whilst the sobs shake their way through me like so many depth charges.

'Look, this really isn't good for you, not in your condition. And I'm sure whatever it was was nowhere near as bad as you think.'

Slowly the tremors subside, and gradually I'm able to talk. I tell it all, as it was. I spare myself nothing. The nicknames, the juvenile fantasy of being in love with one's teacher, the petty revenge of sabotaging her reputation. The district nurse hears me out. When the words come, they're considered, wiser than I have any right to expect.

'Mr. Nicholls, I don't know that I can thank you for telling me all that. I was probably only about six at the time, but I remember them having those jobs, and I liked it living there. What you did was wrong – you don't need me to tell you that. People like my mum and Nicola went through some tough times back then. Attitudes have changed a lot these last twenty years or so, but I knew, growing up, that it was a battle for them, that it made them stronger, made their love stronger. But look, there's something you ought to know. When they left that school it was because Nicola had been head-hunted, there was a job lined up for her in the Sports Faculty at Loughborough Uni. That's where we grew up, me and my sister. Mum gave up her job and went too, because that's what love makes you do. It was nothing to do with you, and your horrible little rumours, nothing at all.'

The air is still between us. She finishes packing her bag. She looks at me again.

'My colleague Dawn will be coming in a couple of days to carry on taking care of you. Don't worry – it's not because of anything you've just said. It was planned anyway – you're doing fine, and I've got other cases that need my time now. But look' – she lays a hand on my arm again, cool this time, distant – 'I don't think I'll tell my mum any of this. I don't think she'd appreciate it. But if I've helped you get this off your chest, then it's a good thing. Just forget it now. You have other things' – she lays a hand gently on my wound – 'to think about.'

She picks up her bag.

'Take care of yourself, Mr. Nicholls,' she says. 'I'll see myself out.'

I sit for a long time, watching the shadows slide across the wall beside me. Forget it? Seems unlikely. It's one thing to know that you aren't the instrument of someone else's destiny. But that gives me no comfort, it doesn't change my motivation from back then – in fact the irrelevance of my actions all those decades ago only makes my shame burn the stronger. I'd like to have seen her again, Pancake Day, to thank her for her kindness to me, to apologise for the way I sullied her name. But the blessing, the secular absolution, of her step-daughter will have to do. It's more than I deserve.

Alien Invasion

As he stares out over the headland, he is aware for what he knows will be the last time of the fading of the light. Darkness has gathered in pools under trees and in the lee of the wall. It has spread across the space where Claudia had the servant girls planting vegetables and fruit trees, so that it has become impossible to distinguish one plot from another. Now his eyes can no longer separate sea from sky on the horizon. He can hear the long exhaling sigh on the shore in the bay far below, the lonely cry of gulls tracking homeward as the light fails, and now there is more light in the sky from the millions of stars, while here on land the colours have died to a uniform black. Still he stares out to sea, searching, waiting. This is where they will come from, he knows. They are not here yet, but they are coming, these invaders, out of the darkness beyond the horizon. What happens when they arrive is, he reflects ruefully, anyone's guess.

He is aware of a sound behind him. Tensed, he reaches for his belt, but something in the footfall tells him it is only Senicianus, here to bid him good night. For a moment they stand side by side, staring out into the blackness.

'Any sign?' Senicianus asks him.

'Not yet,' he replies.

'But they are coming – they *will come*?'

It sounded like a question, but he knows Senicianus knows the answer before the words have formed on his lips.

'Yes, they will come,' he says.

It is a matter of fact, of inevitability. All that is left to know is when. He turns to face his old servant, long since freed from bondage and now the last tie he has left with his military life.

'You are afraid?'

Again, it sounds like a question, though they both know the answer.

'Truthfully?' Senicianus asks. 'Then yes, I am afraid. Their reputation goes before them. I have heard report of their invasions elsewhere in the empire. The slaughter. The wanton destruction of all that we hold dear. The end of civilisation, they call it. It is dark now. Soon there will be darkness even during the hours of day.'

'And the people,' he asks the old man. 'They blame me? They blame us? For not protecting them. For our –' the word sticks a little in his throat – 'for our retreat?'

Senicianus makes no reply. The silence is its own answer. It weighs heavily on both of them. Then Senicianus stirs.

'It is in the hands of the gods,' he says.

Marcus notes wryly that for all the fashion for the new religion of Christianity, the old ways endure. Senicianus continues.

'If I may venture a suggestion, sir, I would advise you to get some rest. There are long days' journeying ahead of you.'

Marcus makes his way indoors. In one of the rooms off the central cylindrical tower he can hear women weeping. He pays it no attention. At the household shrine he stops, lights a votive offering. He does not know why. Perhaps, as for Senicianus, old habits die hard. Perhaps he seeks protection for the journey. Perhaps, beneath the stoic exterior, he too is afraid of the alien invasion.

Marcus is well read. He keeps Theocritus and Virgil stored in his heart. The pastoral elegy has been one of his favourite genres since his days as a callow student in Rome and, though no-one has ever said this to him, he feels it is a marker of his humanity, his sensitivity in the brutalising world of martial conflict. It is the sense of loss, and of a yearning for consolation in the face of the inevitability of death, that he cherishes. He has a reputation, he knows, as a reserved man, abiding by the rules, sober even at a Saturnalian feast. He is, he sees, a man made for twilights, for endings, for a dying fall. He is, he reflects with a rueful smile, a man for these times.

He thinks back to the first time he encountered an alien. The experience was oddly anti-climactic. So much like ourselves, was his first thought. The creature was cold, evidently half-starved and brutalised as much by its treatment at the hands of his men as by the barbarism of the code it lived by. He had anticipated being afraid, so much so that he would have cut its throat if it had thrown itself at him, but in the end he felt nothing other than a kind of pity. Yet for all that, he knows that there are thousands more out there, in the darkness beyond the horizon, and that the threat they pose to him and his way of life is existential, and terminal. A managed decline – that is the best that he can offer as consolation to those who depend on him.

He goes through the great hall and into one of the side rooms where Claudia is supervising the packing of their few personal items for the journey ahead. He finds the weeping tiresome, a sentimentality he has had erased from his character by twenty years of military life and nearly the same period here in this finely-appointed villa on the coast. When the appointment came he did not know whether to be offended that he was being put out to grass or honoured at being given the management of this, the finest building of its kind in the whole province – indeed, some said, in the whole of the empire. At his low points he felt like a glorified manager of a luxury hotel. Military leaders would stay over on their way to more northern outposts, and once – no, twice – this site had been more honoured even than that.

The ornate mural on the wall of the great circular hall told the tale of the visit of the Emperor Flavius, though Marcus knew well enough from historians he had read that the visit was an impromptu one caused by Flavius's ill-health, and that the Emperor had died in the great city to the west that he was travelling to. A mosaic on the floor of the atrium depicted the return visit by Flavius's newly-installed son, Constantine, on his way back south to impose his rule on the rest of the empire. But that was nearly a century ago, and Marcus knows that since then his people have been marking time in this province, waiting for the call that must inevitably come to withdraw completely. What pride, what dignity, he asks himself, is there in being the man 'honoured', as his commission put it, to oversee that?

The next morning, after a night populated by dreams of thousands of aliens scaling the cliffs from the bay below and laying siege to his villa and the nearby rag-tag assortment of wooden houses that the native population still live in, he wakes to the absence of a sea view of any sort. The mist is so thick that he only knows the sea is nearby at all from the sound of its breathing. As is his habit, he takes a tour of the site before breakfast, and the talk he overhears is all of alien invasion and fear hangs in the air like a torn tapestry, obscuring the true view whilst depicting images of horror for the imagination to feast on. Even Claudia, as they eat together, is held in its grip. Frustrated, and perhaps a little afraid himself, he takes her to task.

'In all this talk, my dear, of what might be to come, we should not forget that we too were once aliens here, and talked about by the local population with the same sort of fear that you hear in the kitchens and stables and meeting halls today.'

'Oh, but,' she says, 'that is not the same. Here we are amongst friends.'

He smiles, though his eyes are severe.

'Think of the word,' he says. '"*Alienus*". Foreign. Our people have been living in this province for more than three centuries, but we are still foreigners here. We are as alien to Senicianus, or to Cominda, your waiting woman, or to Andecarus in the stables out there, as the alien hordes beyond the sea are to us.'

Before she can object he hurries on.

'This land is more or less at peace, now. And yes, we have taught these people much. But do you think they welcomed us all those years ago, asking us to show them our metalled roads, our grand stone buildings, our central heating in this godforsaken northerly outpost? Assuredly, they did not. They were subdued with the sword, slaughtered into submission. Why do we think the next invasion will be any different?'

'But,' she shrugs, 'it *is* different now. These people here. They are our friends. They are...' She searches for the word. 'They are ... *civilised*.'

For a moment anger flares in his belly. What can she, a woman, know of politics, of diplomacy, of military strategy? But she is his wife, and Marcus knows that he is unusual in trusting her with his thoughts, and wishes to keep it that way.

'Listen,' he says. 'I will tell you what will happen here once we have left. There will be peace – uneasy, compromised, habitual – for a few years. Perhaps as much as a decade. But gradually two things will happen. These people will remember that they are not all the same, that they belong to tribes, that they will compete for the same resources, not share them as – by military power – we oblige them to now. And they will discover that they have forgotten how to fight. The aliens will come. They will destroy –' he sweeps his arm around – 'all this that we have built. There will be – what does that Hebrew writer say? – "darkness on the face of the deep". It will last for many decades.'

He shrugs.

'It is the way of the world.'

He stands.

'We have a long day ahead,' he says. 'We should prepare to depart.'

Within the hour the pack animals are loaded with an assortment of leather bundles and jute bags. Items of pottery poke out at odd angles, which he doubts will survive the journey. Claudia has finished weeping with the servant girls and the old matrons in the kitchen and stands quietly by, waiting for the signal. He has one last tour of the grounds with Senicianus, one last attempt to make something dignified out of this unceremonious retreat. Eventually there are no more words to say. Senicianus kneels before him. Marcus lays his hand on the old man's head. He had freed him many years ago, so this feels less like manumission and more like a benediction. Marcus reflects again on his reputation for taciturnity. For once, he wishes he could find the right words.

'Well,' he says. 'You are on your own now. Make prudent alliances. Govern the people wisely. Remember that justice is better than vengeance.'

So many platitudes, he thinks.

Senicianus appears to know that he has his own part to play, but it is clear that fear of the future disrupts the script. Is it comfort he wants, wonders Marcus, or the brutal truth?

'These aliens, when they come,' Senicianus asks, 'what will they be like?'

'The English?' Marcus answers. 'They are barbarians.'

Remember Me

With apologies to William Shakespeare

And to think the first postcard nearly went in the bin. If only, my sweet, if only, but back then, well, dearie, who would have known it'd have come to this? There I am, sorting out the mail for his lordship, begging his pardon, him being so very anxious about not seeing all those leaflets, you know how it is, Saga Holidays, and discounts for local pizza parlours, and getting your paintwork touched up by a local handyman, not that I'd mind being touched up by a local handyman these days, what with his lordship having lost interest in all that sort of thing it seems.

So anyway, there I am, putting all that in the recycling – he's very particular, his lordship, about recycling. You might guess as much from his acting parts these last twenty years, know what I mean. Talk about dialling it in. But in with all that junk mail and whatnot there's this postcard. Old fashioned picture, might have been an Edwardian holiday snap or suchlike, like a castle and the battlements, all windswept and moody. So anyway, I turn it over, and there it is, neat as copperplate but enigmatic as a sphinx. 'Remember me?' it says. Just that.

So, I think to myself, mine is not to reason why, and when it's his lordship's lunch time I take it up on the tray and all and offer it to him with a bow and a flourish – he likes all that stuff, gets him in the mood for a bit of the old you know what in the afternoon, or at least it used to before he went off it all – and I say, 'Well, your maj, what do you make of all that?'

He takes the postcard from me, turns it over and over, stares at the handwriting for a bit, clears his throat, and says, 'I'll have a look at that later, my good fellow. And now, to luncheon.'

He's like that. 'To luncheon.' 'What televisual delights have we in store today?' 'A most efficacious tincture.'

And that 'my good fellow'. Who does he think he's kidding? Thirty years ago it was love, darling, love at first sight. First grope, anyway.

'We know what we are, but know not what we may be,' he said, as we headed off out of the stage door and to his hotel room.

Well, let me tell you, old chum, we know what we are now, all right. Gentleman companion to an old queen, that's what. Sometimes, old chum, I don't know why I still put up with it, although he always says there'll be a certain something for me in his will.

So, I come back later to clear up his tray of stuff and what do you know, dearie, but the old dame's mopping his eyes like there's no tomorrow.

'What's up, sweetheart, something in your tea?' I ask, keeping it casual like.

'Here,' he says, holding up the postcard.

'Secret admirer?' Chance'd be a fine thing.

'Do you know where it is?' he asks, pointing at the picture. It's obvious that I don't so he says, 'Elsinore, my dear boy. The scene on the battlements. "Remember me," as the old ghost says.'

'Looks like you've seen one yourself,' I say to him, still playful. 'Still, haven't signed their name, have they? So we'll never know, will we? Unless...'

Unless. Well, yes, there you go, sweetie. Whatever it was got the old water-works working, it doesn't take long for us to go through the whole matinee show again, when the next card comes. Several ladies in nuns' habits – or chaps in drag, more my sort of thing.

'Get thee to a nunnery,' he says, quoting the back of the card, as I bring him his afternoon tea. And then, the week after that, another one with a picture of a courtroom on it, someone holding up a bible in the witness box. 'To thine own self be true,' it says on the back. Never a signature, but enough to put his lordship off his fodder for days on end.

So eventually, what with him tearing up all the time, and me moping about the place like even if I farted out of turn it'd set him off again, I reckon it must be time for a little heart to heart. Aye, there's the rub. It all comes tumbling out, then, as these things must, if you ask too many questions. Of course, he makes a proper performance out of it. If there'd been scenery to chew, you know it wouldn't have gone unmolested. And give the old queen his due, it's pure theatre, the lot of it, but he really knows how to put on a show. The play's the thing, like he always says.

He gathers all the postcards together and says to me, 'When sorrows come, they come not single spies, but in battalions.'

I must look a bit blank, because he goes on.

'One thing after another, dear boy. All these postcards, with their teasing messages. I didn't think she had it in her.'

She? I pride myself in being the soul of discretion, and I've never wanted to shine too bright a light into the orifices of his lordship's past, if you'll pardon the expression, dearie, but you could have knocked me down with a feather boa to think that his past might have contained a woman. A chorus line of male dancers, the odd MP and even the occasional archbishop, maybe, but a woman? It's against nature.

It's possible I let my jaw drop for a little too long, because his lordship says, 'There are more things in heaven and earth, Horatio, than are dreamt of in our philosophy.

You may find it hard to imagine, dear boy, but there was a time when I was a young fellow, when I was less sure than I might be now about, what is it those televisual programmes are so keen on, my orientation and whatnot, and there was indeed a young woman in my past. In my closet, if you will. My own little Ophelia.'

He pats the postcards on the table beside him.

My turn to speak, obviously.

'Well, ok, we all make mistakes. You were young, and people were a bit less open in the olden days' – this said with a smile, so he knows I'm pulling his leg – 'and people in the public eye needed a good cover story.'

He offers me one of his famous wan smiles, the sort that made him everybody's matinee idol back in the day, and shakes his head.

'Something is rotten in the state of Denmark,' he says. 'I don't know what she wants, but I fear we are about to find out.'

And find out we do. More tears, obviously. She comes to pay him a visit. They take tea in the afternoon. At least, I don't think there's anything more going on. Have my ear to the door, naturally, old chum – don't want to find myself suddenly out on my previously cherished posterior, now, do I? But they keep the talk low, so I wait until after I've shown her out, making sure to let her know just how much her presence in our midst has been appreciated, and then hot-foot it up to his lordship, on the pretext that he might want another cup of tea and maybe a drop of the hard stuff, just to calm his nerves and all.

Later, tea drunk and eyes regretfully dabbed, he takes the opportunity to unburden himself. He doesn't take much prompting. It seems that all those years ago, when he and poor sweet Ophelia were engaged in their little dalliance – 'country matters, dear boy, country matters', he says to me by way of explanation – she turned out to be up the duff, in the vernacular, was dropped by her agent, theatres wouldn't touch her with a barge pole, and now, what with one thing and another, and money for her and the poor little runt she brought into the world being in short supply, she'd quite like a finger in his pie, in a manner of speaking.

Only room for the fingers of one of us in there, that's my view, so I try to move the talk on to what we can do to bring this to a rousing climax. Preferably one in which the heroine falls to her death from an upper storey window, or drowns in a passing brook, or some such. Of course, I'd never suggest such a thing directly to the old dame, but there are ways of insinuating that, in a manner of speaking, his little Ophelia could be offered some encouragement to back off, perhaps with a view to it being better for her health, all things considered.

'We should be cruel only to be kind, is that what you're saying?' he asks, a little more obtusely than I'd usually give him credit for. 'One may smile and smile, and be a villain, eh?'

I incline my head with practised gravity. Perhaps we're all *actors* in the end, it seems.

'You're a fine upstanding sort of fellow,' he says to me, giving the old knee a good squeeze. For a while I think maybe we're auditioning for a *Carry On...* film, but there's no 'Ooh, Matron!' moment, and it's obvious that his gratitude doesn't stretch as far as a turn around the old mattress.

I make a few calls – it would be fair to say, my dear, that I've got a few friends in low places – and set the wheels in motion. We wait. His lordship is anxious. But the postcards stop, for a while, and his lordship and I settle quietly into our old routine.

'Though this be madness, yet there is method in it,' says his maj when I update him on the absence of postal communication. 'The lady doth protest too much, methinks.'

One afternoon he even gets his hopes up to the extent that we manage a quite satisfactory bit of slap and tickle after his post-luncheon nap.

But all good things, as they say. I remember the moment vividly, that sense of 'before' and 'after'. I'm polishing the silver in the scullery, as you do, my dear, when the phone rings.

I always put on my best camp posh voice and say, 'Hello, Sir Laurence's ancestral hall, to whom do we have the pleasure?' at times like this, but the voice at the other end says, 'Alright, nancy boy, cut the crap. Need to talk to him indoors. Like, pronto.'

'Ooh, very masterful today, aren't we?' I say, channelling my inner Kenneth Williams, but all he says is, 'Shut it. Get him on the blower, now. Let's just say I've got news for him.'

So, I put the call through to his lordship, but given that there's no keyhole for me to put my ear to this time, I have to wait until luncheon, dear boy, to find out the score. And luncheon, as I'm almost expecting, is somewhat derailed. He's in tears, and it takes many theatrical flourishes and a great deal of waving of his silk handkerchief, before I can get the full story in all its technicolour vividness.

It seems that Mr. Tabloid Editor (I refuse to sully myself by stooping so low as to name names) wishes his lordship to know that this coming Sunday his splendid organ will be publishing, with extensive and salacious detail, the full story not just of his maj's relationship with the no longer quite so shy and retiring Ophelia, but a whole lifetime of misdemeanours, hypocrisies, temper tantrums and (you can imagine the heavy breathing at this point) sexual indiscretions that my employer and, dress it up how you will, my life companion has committed during several decades in the theatre, and associated dressing rooms and hotel bedrooms.

I have never seen a man age quite so dramatically as his lordship does in the five days before Sunday's big reveal. With every breakfast tray, elevenses, luncheon dear boy, afternoon tea with an especially enticing slice of tiffin, and evening meal with the regular preliminary G&T and nightcap to follow, he shrinks faster than a detumescent organ caught in the act in the public conveniences in Covent Garden. I'm sorry, dearie, it's in my nature to be flippant (it's what he fell for in the first place – well, that and my vital statistics), but I have to say, we both weep many salt and bitter tears over those days. Some afternoons he just lies in my arms, sighing, 'O, that this too too solid flesh would melt,' until I become more and more convinced that he has given up the ghost.

Even my best endeavours – 'What a piece of work is man,' I proclaim, inviting him to inspect every inch of me – turn out not to be enough.

By Friday evening he is desolate. I find him, as I bring his nightcap, not tucked up in bed but rifling through the many cabinets in the bathroom, squinting at labels, setting up a little pile of bottles and bubble strips by his shaving mirror.

'Well?' I ask, fearing the obvious.

He takes my hand, and places it against his heart. The action makes me want to crack a joke or find some risqué quip to defuse the emotion. But all he says is, 'There is nothing either good or bad, but thinking makes it so.'

I follow him back to bed. He seems confused, or at least more agitated than I've seen him for some time, so I lie beside him, chaste as one of those nuns on Ophelia's postcard. After a while, his talk turns to death. I don't recognise or understand a lot of it – I guess I've always been his bit of rough, and not one of those luvvies the straight world parodies – but when he's drifting off to sleep, mumbling about 'the undiscovered country from whose bourn no traveller returns' I'm glad we've turned off the light so he can't see my tears. And he's supposed to be the 'sensitive plant', not me!

On Saturday he is, as he says, putting his affairs in order. I want to make jokes – 'hope I'm straight in at number one, then' I say, sashaying over to him – but the matinee idol smile is gone. He talks slowly, methodically, about legal documents, names and addresses of solicitors, distant relatives.

'Don't worry,' he says, 'I haven't forgotten you.'

It takes an effort of will I didn't know I had to ask, 'What ... what will you do?'

The smile comes back, briefly.

'Painkillers. I still have what's left from my knee operation, and that time I had surgery on my slipped disc. Alcohol. You remember Judy Garland. And, oh, what was her name? That diva we used to listen to together. Whitney.'

I can't help myself. 'And I ... will always love you.' I never could sing in tune, and it's pure saccharine drivel, but dangerously honest for a rogue like me.

'Yes, well, my good fellow, a sentiment I wholeheartedly reciprocate. Remember me, won't you, when it's all done. But now it's time for me to take a good, long, slow bath. You won't need to bring my tea in the morning, my boy. I'll lock my door from the inside. Just leave it the right length of time and then ring the authorities. They'll do the rest.'

How simple life is when you strip it down to its bones. We kiss – slow, innocent, the purest kiss I've had in all my whole disreputable life – and I don't want to let him go.

'Go on, boy,' he says. 'Time for me to sleep.'

I pull the door closed behind me, rest my forehead against its rough grain.

'Goodnight, sweet prince,' I whisper, as I turn away and, one by one, douse the remainder of the lights in the house.

The rest, as they say, is silence.

On the Canvas

A fiction, based on 'Le Déjeuner sur l'herbe'
by Édouard Manet

On the canvas the four figures look small from here at the back of the gallery, though the picture is by far the largest on display, at two metres high and nearly two and a half wide. The crowds swarm greedily, hungry for a glimpse, drinking in the scandal. I wait, watching the effect. Portly matrons purse their lips, so many sour cherries. Fastidious critics peer through monocles, pronounce in disparaging tones. Young men gawp at the image, nudge each other, sniggering. Daughters of the middle-classes are gently led away before their innocence is lost forever. Le tout Paris is aghast. I smile, inscrutable behind my high-collared blouse and my fan. Slowly, having supped their fill of seeming horrors, the crowds thin, and I can get close enough to examine his work for myself, though I've known its gestation for the best part of a year now.

Ferdinand leans on his left elbow, soberly dressed though with that funny padded hat that he refused to take off, in or out of doors. He is waving his right arm, making a point to Édouard's brother, who looks exactly what he is, stolid, bourgeois, sensible, dull. With their fobs and watch chains, their scrupulously starched collars, their earnest, sober jackets, they look as though this picnic lunch in the Bois de Boulogne is the height of tedium. In the background, poor

Suzanne is bathing her feet. But nobody is looking at her. They are looking at me. I sit with my chin resting on my right hand, right leg bent through ninety degrees, left leg crooked underneath me. Looking directly out at all those petty scandalised Parisian mothers and aunts, I am wearing a gaze of enigmatic, amused superiority, and nothing else at all.

*

On the canvas there isn't even a mark.

'Good as new,' he says, standing back a little to inspect it.

'There are three more,' I say, indicating downstairs where they're stacked against the wall by the door. 'All in the same condition. I can get you more whenever you want them.'

He looks at me over the rim of his palette. I can see a question starting to form in his mind, so to forestall it I put my bag down on the table and start getting out the food I've brought. There are four small bread rolls and a large baguette, some peaches in a waxy carton, cheese in tissue paper tied up with a ribbon, a bottle of red wine and two glasses wrapped in a silk scarf to keep them safe, and a tray of steamed asparagus with a garlic mayonnaise dressing. I wasn't sure about the last of these, but the man said it was today's most popular dish so I bought it anyway.

I look around the studio for somewhere for us to sit. Édouard doesn't seem to have any space free of all his clutter. I notice there are some weather-beaten old wooden chairs stacked against the wall by the door, set two of them down beside the table, lay out my provisions and sit down, carefully, on one of the chairs. I motion him to do the same. He looks back at me again. The question is still there, in his mind.

'You're –' he says.

'Yes. I'm very kind. I know,' I say back.

I look at him, all the time. Eye contact matters so much. Especially now, especially at this point, especially at the beginning, when everything is so new, and so fragile between us.

'Look,' he says, 'er –'

'Victorine,' I say, maintaining my gaze.

I hold out a hand and he kisses it. I make sure to linger just that moment longer than he is expecting, and as he takes his hand away I brush his cheek gently with my fingertips. I offer him my best smile.

'You artists,' I say, 'you are all the same. Poor famished creatures, starving in garrets, slaves to your muse. You must be fed. You must be nourished. Here.'

I unwrap the wine glasses and proffer the bottle to him. He rummages in a drawer by the sink, finds a corkscrew, eases out the cork and sets the bottle on the table before us. I take it up quickly, before he can offer, pour out two glasses and hand him one. I propose a toast.

'To art,' I say. 'To your art, and to inspiration.'

*

On the canvas, the work is taking shape, though there are signs even now of areas painted over and rearranged. The food spread in the foreground has gone through several versions already, from a depiction that looked like a Renaissance still life, all game birds and platters of fruit, to something much more functional, a simple picnic for the two couples who have wandered out into the woods and stopped for lunch, spreading a rough woollen blanket on the forest floor. In the centre of the picture but set a little into the background is Suzanne, wearing a loose silk chemise. She is bathing her feet in the shallows by the riverbank, as though she might be some classical nymph new to these suburban surroundings. In the foreground, the two men and the other woman are sitting, waiting, it seems, for her to dry her feet and join them. The men talk, earnestly – politics, no doubt, or the stock market – while the sitting woman is bored. I am exactly as Édouard posed me. It is not what I want. It is time to take control.

I'm still not entirely sure why I chose Édouard. He thinks it was an accident – 'What happy chance was it that brought you to my studio that day?' he asks – but it was my plan from the outset. Some things about him – that easy aristocratic bearing that he inherited from his mother, perhaps – might not have marked him out from other aspiring artists with a modicum of talent and the means to indulge it, wanting to be the next Goya or Velazquez. But I saw in that early canvas, *The Absinthe Drinker*, the work of a painter who wanted to provoke, to shock, if only he knew what weapons to use. So the 'accidental' meeting at the entrance to his studio, the chance conversations about canvases and materials, the offers of assistance with his, it has to be said, untidy record-keeping and administration – they have made me, in the two months since that impromptu meal of bread and cheese and wine in his cluttered studio, not just his assistant but his model. And soon, as I intend, his muse.

He makes me a drink of bitter black coffee and we share a pastry, staring out across the steep rooftops of Paris from the high windows of his studio. The wintry light is a cold, clear blue, but inside the studio it is barely warmer than out there on the street. The painting is not going well. We talk, carefully, of his intention, of the contrast between the three sturdy Parisian middle-class day-trippers and the exotic figure of the pastoral bather in the middle distance. It is a nice idea – to highlight the dreariness of mundane reality by showing a glimpse into the world of classical myth – but the result is stubbornly earthbound. He wants me to try sitting in a range of different postures so that I guide the viewer's eye back to the woman bathing. Sometimes I look straight at her. Other times I am in profile, as though listening to Ferdinand as he drones on and on.

As he paints, and as I shiver in the heavy, respectable shawl he has me wear, we flirt idly. He issues instructions. 'Look more like you have just been kissed,' he says. It has been like this for some weeks, but today it is tinged with tension caused by the impasse on the canvas. Finally he throws down his brushes with an oath, tells me we are done for the day. The frustration is tangible. There is a thundercloud waiting to burst. He heads downstairs to the urinal. I tell him I will clean his brushes and let myself out.

As soon as he leaves the room, I make my move. Quickly I throw off the sombre shawl, the sober, respectable matronly boots I am wearing, peeling away the layers of propriety. It is so cold I could strike a match on my goose-pimples. My nipples are hard and erect. I can barely stop my teeth chattering. But when he comes back upstairs I am ready for him, naked, sitting still in profile but now with my head facing him directly at the top of the stairs, smiling, confrontational, in control.

The effect is like a thunderclap. He is but a man, after all. We make love, hungrily, a release from the frustration of the day. In that act, so basic and primitive, I am stronger than he. His climax comes only when I permit it, when he knows that I am in control. Afterwards, rather to my surprise, he is full of apology, as though he has taken advantage of me. It is as if he hasn't understood what has happened, but he will.

*

On the canvas the story of the luncheon on the grass is taking shape. Off it, Édouard has become that rather sweet thing, my attentive lover. Each morning in the studio we make love, hungry for each other the way we will later fall on the pastries and cold meats and fruit of our breakfast. He looks at me with a painter's eye, watching the way my body moves, the curve of my thigh, the way my hair falls across my face, the way I lie before him, open and unashamed. I can see that he is composing paintings of me in his mind.

Now, when I pose for him, the focus of the picture has shifted, so that its weight is in the foreground. Partly it is in my nakedness, in the shock of my body against the stuffy respectability of the two men, still engaged in their talk of financial markets or the looming threat of political collapse, as though I were invisible to them, as though I did not exist at all. Ferdinand still sits across from me in the image. If he wanted, he could examine my body, read the meaning in my breasts, the promise of the future nestled between my thighs. Now the focus is no longer on poor Suzanne, bathing chastely in the background. That was art, her pose seems to say. That was art, but this is life.

But it is not just the fact of my nudity. After all, as Édouard reminds me as we lie back, breathless, the sweat cooling on our skin, on the threadbare rugs spread out on his studio floor, women have been nude in paintings for centuries, their bodies displayed for men to admire. And this, I tell him, is why I am here.

'We have wandered round the Louvre so many times,' I say. 'Have you tried counting how many women in these paintings, even the respectable ones by Raphael or Mantegna, are naked? And then try counting the naked men.'

My hands form weighing scales, mimicking the weight in one pan, the lack of it in the other.

He smiles.

'Art is made by men,' he says.

Something in me stirs at that, its casual assumption of territory, but I can't deny the fact of it, much as I want to dispute its meaning.

'And art is commissioned by men, bought by men, displayed by men in their villas and chateaux and galleries,' he goes on. 'Don't they have a right to choose what they look at, to look at what they enjoy?'

The smile is still there on his lips. I'm only joking, it seems to be saying. Or at least, only a little. And then he makes his ultimate mistake.

'After all,' he says, 'I chose you.'

It is like a flare going off in my brain. With a snarl I swipe the half-drunk coffee from his unsuspecting hand, sending the cup splintering across the floorboards. I lever myself upwards, straddle him, grip his jaw in my hand to extinguish the trace of a smirk still playing there.

'Look at me,' I insist. 'Look at me, straight into my eyes.'

For a moment I can see that he thinks we are still at play, and he stiffens beneath me in this erotic game. But I hold him with my gaze, intent, focused, dominant. He wilts under me, under the force of my power.

'Édouard,' I say. 'Do not forget this moment. This is the moment when you will understand that you did not choose me. I chose you.'

I watch his eyes flicker. For a second he is a small boy caught in a trespass. I wonder if I have said too much, if he will not be strong enough to understand the new reality. I slip sideways, lie on my side, propped on elbow and hip, and with my other hand I trace a line slowly with my fingertip down his naked torso. He is watching me, watching my eyes.

I kiss him, chastely, on the cheek, and smile.

'Édouard,' I say, 'it is all right. We chose each other.'

I gesture to where the painting stands, incomplete.

'This is your art,' I say. 'Only you could make it. But you could not make it this way without me.'

*

On the canvas my finished pose retains that look of amused superiority that Édouard saw that day. The fools at the Paris Salon refused to exhibit it. It is their loss. The success of the painting at the Salon des Refusés, a 'succès de scandale' no doubt, cemented Édouard's place as the foremost young painter of the day. Many pages of print have been wasted in searching it for meaning in the days since it went on display. I am nothing but a common tart, I am to understand. I am an image of corruption, of the shallow crudity of feckless youth, of the loss of taste and respectability in this new generation.

Bah! These people do not trust their eyes. They cannot read. If I were smiling at Ferdinand, and at Édouard's pompous brother, they might have a case for saying I am there merely to meet the feeble needs of men. If my eyes were downcast, a blend of the demure and the ashamed, stripped of my dignity in masculine company, they might have a point in claiming that I am merely humiliated.

But look at me. Look at my face. Look into my eyes. What you can read there is a challenge thrown down. On the canvas I can scorn the scandalised masses. And you, I ask the observer, walking demurely round the gallery? What do you think? But then, what you think does not matter. My strength can face you down as well.

Girl with Fan

His words echo through my mind, even now, more than five decades later.

'Alphonsine Fournaise, I picked you out. I could have had anybody,' he said, back in 1881. I remember it as though it were yesterday. 'You know what you were back then? A waitress. If you've made a name for yourself since, it's down to me.'

What was I supposed to do? Carry on being grateful to him, the renowned Pierre-Auguste, when it was obvious he'd moved on, to that shallow little hussy of a dressmaker that took my place when barely more than a child, in his studio and in his bed. At least he had the decency to put a ring on her finger – eventually, when their snotty little bastard was five years old already. But I've had the last word. Still here at ninety-one, though as I said to Claudine when she came to help me dress this morning, I don't expect to see out another winter. The world's turning dark, in any case, and I don't want to live through another war.

I peer over at the newspaper she left on my dressing table, where it sits beside the fan that nobody will ever remove, that will lie beside me in my coffin. 3rd December, 1936. The date nags away for a moment, until at last I remember. The date of his death, seventeen years ago now. I remember going to see him when he was dying, to that house that he kept like a shrine to the memory of that dumpy little petit-bourgeois housewife she turned into. At first he refused to let me into his bedroom, but I put that stupid maid of his in her place and shouted through the closed door, 'What do you mean, you don't need me?'

That was enough for him to let me in. Did we kiss and make up? Hah! What do you think? I just wanted to see him, dying, and for him to know that he might have stolen my youth and my innocence, but that I'd been counting the days until I could see him in his grave. You may think me bitter, and there are those who suggest that it's unhealthy to bear grudges, but that's what's kept me alive all these years. And now I can tell my tale, our tale, without fear of challenge or contradiction.

*

At first we didn't know why Papa bought the land by the Seine downstream of Paris. Later my brother said it was probably to give him something to do after Maman died. 1857, as I recall. I must have been about eleven when the building went up, and within weeks, it seemed, of *La Maison Fournaise* opening to the public, the people flocked to us to eat, drink and enjoy the extraordinary light reflected off the river. I remember Papa fretting a little about the sort of clientele we were attracting, but as Mathilde, the tough old Parisienne he employed to manage front of house, said to him, what does it matter who they are as long as they pay up and don't cause fights. The artists arrived first – somewhere to drink and gossip and flirt between sessions painting by the river – and they drew with them the rest of that sort of bohemian crowd: actresses, poets, musicians, and all their hangers-on. I should give Papa his due. He knew a good employee when he saw one, and the kitchen staff produced good, economical food at speed, and an excellent selection of homely wines to wash it down.

Strangely, given his subsequent fame, it was his voice that I first noticed. After a long, leisurely lunch, or as dusk fell over the tables, someone would call out for a song, and his sturdy tenor held the listeners captive, with much applause and back-slapping to follow.

'Who is that young man?' I asked my brother.

'That?' he asked. 'That's Pierre.' He thought for a little. 'Pierre-Auguste Renoir. He's having singing lessons, I believe, though he earns so little it wouldn't keep a church mouse alive, so God knows how he can afford it.'

At busy times Papa had me waiting at table as soon as he saw I could keep track of an order from beginning to end. So I had plenty of opportunity to catch his eye as I served the dishes or cleared away at the end of a meal. Sometimes I stood as if in a trance, mesmerised by the flow of gossip, most of which I didn't understand, and he'd raise his hand and click his fingers at me to jolt me out of my dream.

'Ah,' he'd say, with a smile to the others at the table, 'it's la petite rêveuse, the little dreamer.'

And as I piled the dirty plates and balanced them on my forearm, he rested a hand on my hip, where the touch burned as though his fingers were aflame.

The history of seduction is a long one, but, let's face it, the strategies in play are limited. Sometimes he brought his mistress with him, a blowsy brunette given to laughing too easily, and I didn't like him so much then. But she appeared less and less often and one day, as I was bringing another jug of wine, one of those sitting with him proposed a toast: 'To the single life!' and he threw his head back and drank, with an 'Amen to that!'

And after that, there was always occasion to loiter a little as his friends made their way out of the restaurant, and share a few words – a compliment on my waitressing skills, perhaps, or a remark about how well the cut of my dress suited me. As for me, I was tongue-tied for the most part, but took the compliments with a blush and a smile that I hoped signalled sophistication, though I suspect it communicated only the callow innocence of my years.

Still, he told me things.

'I am studying to be an artist now,' he said, once. 'They say I have talent, but I don't know about that. But I must practise, always practise.'

And then he said, as if the thought had just struck him, 'Perhaps you would like to sit for me sometime. It would be a privilege to try to capture the freshness and purity of youth.'

I must have blushed even more than normal, because he said, 'If your Papa will allow it, of course. And if he can spare you from your duties here, which I see keep you occupied.'

Another smile, and a hand on my arm, but casually brushing against my breast.

'And how old are you, Alphonsine?'

'Fifteen,' I said. 'That is, sixteen ... soon.'

'Admirable,' he said. 'As a young man of nineteen – that is, twenty ... soon – I would consider it an honour if you would sit for me. We shall consult your Papa.'

*

There are a number of portraits, naturally, but as with so many other things in life, in this too there was necessarily the first one. For years I had no idea what had happened to that painting. It seemed to have disappeared, and certainly I never saw it in any of the exhibitions in Paris over the years. I wondered if he'd destroyed it, as though – and I knew I was lying to myself even as I thought it – as though the very act of looking at it would remind him of his heartlessness towards me, and when it all began.

But there was a posthumous exhibition, in New York of all places, and someone happened to have brought back a catalogue from the exhibition, and there it was. *Girl with Fan*, it said underneath the image, and then '(Date unknown)'. That made me laugh. I could have told them, down to the hour almost, when that painting was finished. 5pm, April 13th, 1862. By rights it was one of the earliest of his paintings to have survived, part of what they now call his juvenilia, and it predated everything else in that New York exhibition by nearly five years.

He had a little studio down by the river. A damp, draughty place, full of the smell of decay in summer, bitterly cold in winter. But in spring – in April, say – the light glowed off the peeling whitewashed walls as though the building were animate, and lit from inside by its own life force. The first time I went there we talked about how I might pose, what felt natural, what made me feel awkward. The truth was, I had no idea. The thought of being the focus of such intense concentration made me squirm inwardly.

'Come,' he said, 'you're "la rêveuse" – yes? So just … daydream.'

There were things I wouldn't – couldn't – do, like wear some of the mythical costumes he kept in a kind of threadbare dressing-up box in one corner. Some of them showed too much of me for me to feel confident even putting them on, let alone allowing him to see me in them. Then how to stand, or sit; how to look, or where; what to do with my hands. He despaired of ever getting me to stand poised for long enough to fix the pose on canvas, so he sat me in a plain armchair in one corner of the room. Eventually he gave me a fan that was lying on a bench with some hats and shawls and an odd umbrella, and I opened it in front of me like a protective barrier.

And so we began.

'Don't look so worried, ma petite,' he said. 'Nothing will happen except what you want to happen.' And then, though I didn't know I wasn't, he said, 'And smile. Imagine you have an armful of plates!'

I laughed, and the ice was broken.

As I say, the manual of seduction has very few chapters. I'd watched him and his friends flirting at the restaurant, and I knew the moves in the game, even if I'd never played it myself. The exaggerated eye contact; the flourish in kissing my hand at the end of a session; his hands resting longer as he put my cloak around my shoulders, his fingers brushing my cheek; a faint, fleeting kiss on my forehead like a benediction. But the first time is always raw, shocking, a violation.

The painting was declared finished. We stood before it, his arm round my waist, drawing me towards him. He kissed me, on the lips – nobody had ever done that before, and I had no idea how to react – and then he took me by the hand and said, 'Come, we should celebrate,' and he led me to the curtained-off area at the back of the studio, where a roughly made bed stood waiting. I felt as though I were in a trance, and I let him do what he wanted to do, though it hurt so much and the blood frightened me, but when I went home that evening, all I could think was, 'And now I am going to be Mme. Pierre-Auguste Renoir, wife of the famous painter.'

I was a child, and a foolish one at that.

*

I still have the fan, of course. It sits on my dressing table and nobody touches it except me. It's a memento. Not, I suppose, a memento mori, though in some ways perhaps it is, in that death is pregnant in us from the moment of inception, is it not? To be frank, for the first few days that followed the world churned around me. I got a good few scoldings from Mathilde for mixing up orders, and customers demanding discounts for having to wait too long. For two days he did not appear with the rest of the crowd and I was sick with fear that he'd found somewhere else, someone else. Then when he did appear, it was as though he wouldn't acknowledge me, as if I had become invisible.

But after one long, leisurely lunchtime, as his friends said their farewells, he stopped me by the door to the kitchens and said, 'I am going to the theatre tonight. Come with me, Alphonsine. I want to be seen with you.'

For a moment I was sick with a cocktail of hope, fear and anxiety.

'But Papa?' I said, with a sense of inevitability.

'I will speak with your father,' he said, as though that would settle it. But, to my astonishment, it did. I don't know what Papa made him promise, but Papa was nothing if not a pragmatist, ready to accept changes to any situation and to see how best to make them work to his advantage.

And so began my years of dreaming. I was 'la rêveuse' still, but in a dream from which I never wished to wake. New worlds opened up before me, places I'd never visited before, social occasions that I would have felt dazzled to navigate were it not for the fact that Pierre-Auguste was so evidently proud to have me on his arm. How long does it take for a sixteen-year-old to find her place in the world? It is with pride that I say that the metamorphosis was almost instant, from a gauche waitress at table to a society lady honoured in theatres, ballrooms, cafés and bars across all of Paris.

I suppose in my mind I was, in effect, 'Mme. Renoir', though Pierre-Auguste would never lower himself to something so bourgeois as to propose marriage. We were free souls, he said, paired in flight for as long as we both flew in harmony. It's so odd that I couldn't hear the meaning of that until it was far too late.

After that first portrait, I came to feel no fear in sitting for him, only a burning elation that here I was, being immortalised on canvas. I remember *Lady Smiling*, to which he appended the subtitle *(Portrait of Alphonsine Fournaise)*. The smile is subdued, but my gaze at the viewer secure in possession of my place at the centre of this creation. I must have been twenty-five by then, and already confident that I belonged. My days of waiting at table were fading into the past, and when I visited Papa and my brother and the old crowd at *La Maison Fournaise* it was to be given a place at the finest table, with the best view across the Seine to the far bank, my meal served on the costliest china.

And to Pierre-Auguste I was still, and always, 'La Rêveuse'. In one of the last paintings in which I sat for him, when he was nearly forty and I, I suppose, about thirty-five, I went back to a similar armchair to that first portrait of so many years before, but with no need to hide behind a fan or stare blankly out at the viewer. He called that picture *La Rêveuse*, the Dreamer, and I gaze confidently but still coquettishly out of the canvas at him, little finger teasingly to my lips, dreaming still.

*

If I say that from all dreams, in the end, the sleeper awakes, it is not because I have succumbed to cliché in my old age. It is because the jolt into consciousness is so abrupt that one is forced to realise that the world has moved on whilst one has been slumbering thus. With hindsight I could tell the story without need of explanation, but it was only when I found her nightclothes and underwear for myself that I had to confront the truth. For an instant I almost begged him.

'We've had such good times these past few years,' I insisted. 'So you think you've changed your mind? Well, change it back again or we'll both end up sorry for it.'

At first I thought it didn't matter who she was, or whether she was even the first. But it stung, God how it stung. A mousy little seamstress who was barely twenty years old. An empty-headed girl-child whose only interest was in kittens and lapdogs. We raged for weeks, threats and entreaties, cutting remarks and deafening silences. I went back to *La Maison Fournaise*, talked to my brother. He shrugged at my predicament.

'He's forty years old and a man,' he said. 'He's trying to hold on to his youth.'

The end, inevitably, was a painting. Even now, seventeen years after his death and – let me see – fifty-five years after he painted it, it makes me livid that this should be one of his most lauded works. You will have seen it, no doubt.

Indeed, with advances in printing these past decades, you may have a copy hanging on your living room wall, or furnishing your favourite restaurant. *Luncheon of the Boating Party* he called it, though I know from its artfully constructed design that precious little boating went on. There was scarcely time, what with all the drinking and gossiping and flirting. It's a busy scene, behind that table in the foreground laden with bottles of wine and the debris of the end of a fine meal. All his old friends are there, all dead now, as far as I know – the poet Jules Laforgue, the painter Gustave Caillebotte, the actress Jeanne Samary, and all the rest.

I know what he was doing. He was saying, look, this is the in-crowd, the movers and shakers, the people who are not just existing but really living. To the left is my brother, leaning with his back against the café railing and watching over the scene benignly. And there, left of centre but facing the viewer, am I, another passive observer, no longer part of this throng but looking in as though on the other side of the glass, the dreamer to the end. And who am I observing most, down at the front on the left, playing with her little lapdog even though there's food and drink on the table? It is Aline, vacant woman-child, long-time mistress and wife of Pierre-Auguste Renoir, bearer of his children and, so the fawning biographies tell us, love of his life.

*

I make my way as well as my ninety-one years are able over to my dressing table to pick up the fan. It shows the signs of seventy-five years of wear and tear but still, if I unfold it carefully, I can match its design against the image in the New York catalogue of the allegedly anonymous subject of the *Girl with Fan*. I address her directly across the years, ventriloquizing.

'It's time I got on and lived my own life,' I make her say to the world, 'it's what I have to do now.'

The world slips slightly out of focus. As I watch, the image looks a little more closely out at me.

'And have I?' she asks. 'Have you? Have you lived – really lived?'

I choke back a tear, and resume my familiar steely demeanour.

'I have lived,' I say. 'Not just lived. I have outlived them, the whole lot of them.'

'And loved?' the not-yet-woman in the image asks.

'Ah, love,' I say, putting the fan back down on the dressing table and resting my aching bones once more in my familiar armchair. 'Love? Love requires luck, and is not ours to control. We have survived, you and I, and on our own terms. Let that be enough.'

Author's Note:
The sitter for Renoir's 'Girl with Fan' was a young woman called Alphonsine Fournaise. Unusually for Renoir, he didn't append a date to the painting. We know that he painted a rather older Alphonsine a further five or six times during the 1870s, including 'Lady Smiling (Portrait of Alphonsine Fournaise)' (1875) and 'La Rêveuse' (1879). The final painting in which she appears is 'Luncheon of the Boating Party' (1881), which coincidentally is one of the first paintings in which Renoir's mistress and subsequent wife Aline Charigot features.

Almost nothing is known about Alphonsine Fournaise except for her dates of birth and death: 1845-1937. She was four years younger than Renoir. He almost certainly got to know her because her father opened La Maison Fournaise, a bar/restaurant on the banks of the Seine on the outskirts of Paris in 1857. The location was a fashionable meeting place for artists, musicians and other creative figures for several decades, until it closed in the early 20th century.

There is no indication that Alphonsine and Renoir had any kind of intimate relationship.

UFO

The posters line the walls of the old library building. The pull-quotes are excitable. 'A revelation!' – *The Guardian*. 'Kowalski: an undiscovered genius' – *Time Out*. 'Unmissable!' – *The Times*. 'UFO series is a prize-winner in the making' – *Yorkshire Post*. There are others. The artist seems to be the name on everyone's lips, the missing link between Picasso and Basquiat. The art world's heart is obviously aflutter with it all.

I'm not much interested in the art world. But I am interested in Jerzy Kowalski, whose debut major exhibition at the age of 92 is what has brought me to Sheffield for the first time in over thirty years. I look round me, startled at the changes. I recognise the Crucible Theatre from the old days, though its frontage seems to have changed. But in the other direction there's nothing but disorientation: the shiny, glassy upturned hull of the Winter Garden, shiny hotels where I have hazy memories of a hideous Town Hall extension, shiny steel fountains in the Peace Gardens. The old world turned upside down, like something alien has landed from outer space. Seems like a good enough metaphor for what I feel inside.

I asked Ben if he wanted to come.

He spat. 'Sick bastard, he is. Making Mum do all that sort of stuff. Should be hanging him, not his paintings.'

I don't see much of Ben these days. We don't often see eye to eye. On my own, then. I walk up the steps of the Library building, decide to put the moment off by taking the stairs to the fourth floor, and then here I am at the entrance to Graves Art Gallery. Inside, there's the usual sort of crowd, I guess. Not my type, I feel instinctively, without asking myself why. But there he is, on the far side, next to a row of images hanging alongside him, shaking the occasional hand. A bit doddery, ill-fitting suede jacket, wild thicket of flying white hair, even at his age. All these years, but I'd still recognise him anywhere, even after decades. I realise my fists are clenched, and I make myself breathe, relax, loosen the taut muscles of my shoulders and neck. Then I walk towards him.

*

We called him Jersey back then. 1960s. New-ish council flat in Pitsmoor, one of four in a little block, two flats upstairs, two down, with a shared front door and a central lobby with stairs going up to the flats above. We lived on the ground floor on the right. Jersey and Hanna were in the flat above us. We'd got a ground floor flat because of Mum, whose left leg ended just below the knee and who wore a prosthetic limb attached with complicated strapping and buckles. It was never strange to us. It was just Mum – she'd always been like that. Sometimes, just to remind ourselves of the family story, we'd ask her about her leg and what had happened.

'Oh, nothing much,' she'd say. 'I was about your age,' – pointing at Ben who must have been seven or so at the time – 'and someone dropped some big bit of metal off the top of the flats we lived in then and it came flying down out of the sky and hit me on the leg.'

It was never anything special to her, even though I'm ashamed to say that when we were quite a bit older we were often embarrassed being seen walking round town with her.

When we first moved in – me and Ben and Mum (don't ask about Dad; we never did) – it was so exciting. Ben and I didn't have to share Mum's room. The toilet was inside, in a bathroom with a real bath. Heating working all the time, from some central source somewhere. I must have been six, maybe; Ben, two years older. He looked out for me, kept an eye on me at school, though he was in the Juniors and I was still across the playground in the Infants. Mum used to make us tea and we'd watch telly, an old black-and-white, with it on our laps.

'This is the life,' she'd say, arms round us both. And it was.

Jersey and Hanna were already there, upstairs. We were frightened at first. They'd come down the stairs to the front door, talking in a way I didn't understand.

'Polish,' said Mum. 'They're Polish. From Poland.'

It meant nothing to a six-year-old. He wore strange clothes, baggy felt jackets, a soft hat to one side of his head so it slipped over his ear, blotches of paint on his face or his hands or the knees of his trousers. She was stern, smart, a bus conductor. We'd see her sometimes as Mum was taking us to school.

'Morning, Mrs. Kowalski,' Mum would say.

'*Dzien dobry*,' she'd say back, 'Mornink.'

It wasn't just the language that scared us. Upstairs now and then we'd hear shouting, stamping feet, things breaking, then the slamming of doors, more stamping feet in the stairwell outside our door, and one or the other of them stomping off down the path to the road. At night there might be crying, not just crying like when you'd fallen off your bike, but a loud keening sound like all the heartbreak in the world pouring out at once. Mum tried to explain sometimes.

'They were in the war,' she'd say, though apart from the odd film on the telly that didn't really mean anything. 'Lots of bombing, stuff flying down out of the sky, like something coming out of nowhere,' she'd say. 'They had to leave it all behind. Came here with nothing. Sometimes I think they're very sad.'

Some days we'd get home from school and old Jersey would be sitting at the bottom of the stairs, a bottle in one hand, his head resting against the plastered wall, weeping. Mum would shush us to one side, then take him by the arm.

'Come on, Mr. Kowalski,' she'd say. 'Let's get you home,' and then she'd help him up the stairs to his door, slowly because of her leg and his drunkenness, push it open, take him inside, and come back down a minute or two later, smoothing down her coat as she did so.

'What is it, Mum?' we'd ask. 'Why is he like that?'

'He's very upset,' she'd say. 'Apart from his painting, I don't think he knows how to cope.'

I'd been upstairs to his flat once, peering from behind Mum as she brought him some shopping – Hanna must have been out at work – and I could see that the flat was a tip. There were canvases everywhere, a room full of paint and brushes and easels and mess, and old Jersey in ragged old clothes and a smock that was filthy and grey. The pictures didn't look like anything to me – some stick figures but lots of broken things and flashes of colour and odd shapes. Nothing like I'd ever seen in the picture books I was learning to read from.

I don't recall when stuff started coming down from the windows of their flat, but at first me and Ben were both excited, like it was a game or something. It might be a tennis ball, or a shoe, or an old magazine. Not every morning, but often enough for Ben to say, 'Old Jersey's at it again,' peering out of our front room window at the scabby patch of grass in front of the building. We were too scared to take it back up to him, though. You never knew when he might cry, or shout at us in Polish. Mum used to take things back up to him once she'd taken us to school.

I don't know why this didn't strike me as odd at the time – I guess kids just accept that the world is a mysterious place – but part of the game of flying objects was that Mum always seemed to know what they were, even without looking. Sometimes it was the best part of the game. Ben and I would watch from our front room window before it was time for school and something would land on the grass in front of us, not every day, but now and then.

'What is it then, Mum?' we'd shout.

'Erm, a tube of toothpaste?' asked Mum, from the kitchen, and we'd stare at each other, round-eyed and amazed. How did she know? At the time it felt like she had some kind of super-power, like the X-ray specs the cartoon figures wore in those comics Ben used to get.

'A cheese grater?' Wow!

'A plant-pot?' Amazing!

'A pencil case?' It was like having some special gift in the family, that only Ben and I could share in.

Until the day that it wasn't. I can't put a date on this at all, but I must have been about nine when we moved away, and I reckon the flying objects game must have been going on for at least a year. One day a torn painted canvas stretched over a broken frame landed with a heavy thud outside our window. Mum guessed it was a newspaper. Ben and I stared at each other, puzzled.

'Oh,' said Mum. 'A plastic bottle, then.' No.

She tried a few more guesses, randomly, before we brought her into the front room and showed her the mess. The canvas had been followed by another, then another, and finally with a great crash, the splintered frame of a big wooden easel itself. Mum put her hand to her mouth. She was shaking.

'What is it, Mum? What's he doing?' we asked, but before she could answer there was stamping in the stairwell and then a violent thudding at the door.

It was Mrs. Kowalski. We couldn't understand most of what happened, because lots of it was in Polish, but we knew from the tone of her voice that she was angry, very angry, and it wasn't with her husband. It was with Mum.

'You are bitch – filthy bitch!' we heard her shout, and our ears burned as we hid behind the front-room door.

There was slapping, a scuffle, and Mum pushed the door closed. We peered out from where we'd been hiding. She was shaking, and there was a huge red mark on her cheek and a trickle of blood at the corner of her mouth. For a while time seemed to stop, and then I burst into tears. I think Ben must have thought, as the older brother, that he was supposed to be the man of the house, but even he cried too. We were late to school that day.

When we got home, Mum was brisk, matter of fact. We were going to move. She didn't like it here after all. We boys needed separate rooms of our own now we were growing up. She'd put our names down for a new council house. We could have our very own garden. It would be exciting. The days and weeks that followed were numb. No mystery objects came flying down from the flat above to land on the grass outside our window. In fact, it wasn't just quiet in our flat. It was quiet upstairs too. Mrs. Kowalski still went out to do her shifts on the buses, studiously avoiding eye-contact if we overlapped in the communal hallway, and we heard Jersey from time to time, moving furniture around, or his footsteps going to and fro from the kitchen. But we never saw him, and we didn't say goodbye when we moved.

And that was it, as far as I was concerned, for thirty years. We grew up. Ben got a job on a building site, got married, had a kid, then divorced, then married again. I went to university, got an academic librarian job that meant I had to move away. I visited Mum now and then, as she got older and found walking harder and harder, and conversations on the phone seemed more and more confusing to both of us, until one day I got an abrupt call from Ben telling me she'd died. I came back to Sheffield for the funeral, but found nothing to keep me there after the event. There was nothing to link my life in my flat just off campus to those hazy days of my early childhood, and in all honesty I think not a single moment passed for decades when the memories crossed my mind.

It was about a year ago when I was cataloguing some new acquisitions that I came across a rather glossier academic tome than the usual. The image on the front cover made me sit down suddenly, gripping the book that was shaking between my hands. It was a photograph of an old white-haired man, someone who'd obviously made an effort to tidy himself up (or perhaps had been tidied up for the occasion) standing next to an easel on which was a substantial canvas. 'Jerzy Kowalski – Lost Polish Master' proclaimed the title. The image on the canvas was indistinct, but even in that context I could see that in the midst of what looked like a bombing scene, with unidentifiable fragments of buildings or missiles or other sorts of wreckage in the aftermath of the explosion, there was a woman, naked, but flailing her arms, one leg broken off at the knee, the severed limb, or maybe it was a prosthetic one, lying on the ground beside her. I had no doubts as to what, or whom, I was seeing.

I took the book home that evening and, fortified by a whisky or two, read it from cover to cover. It told me some things I already knew, some that I didn't. Jerzy Kowalski was a Polish refugee, arrived in this country at the end of the Second World War, lived in obscurity in rented property in an insalubrious suburb of Sheffield, a widower with no known remaining family, painted incessantly and obsessively, and whose work was only now finding its way into the public gaze. The writer had evidently interviewed Mr. Kowalski, and it was clear from the text that the artist was saying little about his life and the inspirations for his painting. The writer made much of this enigmatic quality, and the mysteries of the creative process. There was one particular tranche of paintings, huge, startling and graphic, which the writer called 'Kowalski's UFO series', with its mystery woman at the centre of them, surrounded by flying debris, sometimes whole, sometimes dismembered, always naked, head thrown back in a vision that could have been anguish or a kind of erotic ecstasy. Extensive research, said the writer, had failed to identify the sitter, the focal point of this great series, but despite Mr. Kowalski's reticence, the writer was sure that this was the artist's muse, his inspiration, possibly (who knew?) his lover.

In the months that followed there were other items about Kowalski in the arts pages of newspapers or cultural magazine programmes on the TV. An exhibition was planned, first in Sheffield in honour of his newfound local celebrity status, then moving to London. I saw an unnerving clip of him being interviewed by Alan Yentob on the BBC News, the camera panning across images of an ecstatic naked woman surrounded by unidentified flying objects before returning to this old man with his rheumy eyes and disorderly white hair. I found out the dates of the exhibition, booked myself some annual leave, and waited.

*

I walk across the space towards him. He is talking to a tall young woman with a clipboard, who makes some notes and heads briskly across to the office area. I seize my chance. Approaching him, I hold out my hand, mustering my best polite smile.

'Mr. Kowalski?' I ask.

He looks a little startled, but shakes my hand, and mutters, 'Yes, yes, I am.'

I try to be casual, interested but not pushy.

'It's a wonderful exhibition,' I say. 'You must be very pleased with all the recognition, after all this time.'

He looks up at me, mistily, and shrugs.

'All this talk,' he says, waving his arm, 'the papers and the television. They mean nothing. Only the art means anything...'

He trails off, exhausted maybe from the effort. I wait a moment then press on.

'These paintings,' I say, pointing to the sequence of eight imposing canvases running along the wall to his left. 'They are extraordinary. So powerful. I wondered' – I let a short pause elapse – 'I wondered if you could tell me a little about them.'

'Oh,' he says, cautious again. 'A long time ago. What does any painting mean? Only what the viewer wants it to.'

I can't wait any longer.

'You see, they interest me because, well because I think I knew the sitter.'

The jolt is immediate. Blood drains from his face and for a moment I think he is going to faint, if not worse. But then he regains his composure. He stares at me again, as if trying to read the code that would make me known.

'Mr. Kowalski,' I say, trembling in spite of myself, 'please. Please answer me. You see' – it's the hardest moment of my life, I think – 'it's my mother.'

The effect on him is instantaneous. He reaches for my hand, draws me with him to a couple of chairs ranged against the wall. We sit. He still has hold of my hand, and I can feel that he is shaking.

'And you are Benjamin, or – or'.

I shake my head.

'Ben is my older brother. But we often wondered, when we lived in that flat below yours, about it, about it all.'

This is all unravelling so differently than I'd planned it in my head. I'd imagined a confrontation, an accusation, an apology. But he's too old, too frail, too lost, for me to even think of being aggressive. Still, there are ghosts to lay to rest.

'Mr. Kowalski, please, if you would, can you tell me something?'

He nods, gesturing openly. 'Of course.'

'There were things that happened, strange things sometimes. Like you would throw stuff out of your upstairs window, and Mum, she would just know. What they were, I mean. I never thought about it at the time, but now, seeing these paintings, was it – well, a code, maybe?'

He smiles, embarrassed perhaps to be caught in the act, but more, I think at the tenderness of the memory.

'Yes, it was as you say. A signal. It is safe to come up. We can paint together, and, and –'

He stops. It is as though the past is real, there within sight of us, as he stares into space.

'Your mother was –' he searches for the word – 'she was extraordinary. Like no-one I have ever met, before or since. A vision. A woman capable of carrying so much meaning, so much...'

There are tears in his eyes. His hand, still gripping mine, is shaking.

'Mr. Kowalski,' I ask, 'were you, were you' – another pause; I can't bring myself to use the word – 'were you … close?'

He looks at me with exhausted eyes.

'Mr. Jennings, it is so very long ago. We knew each other for what, two years? But it was as though' – he gives up on language, makes a whistling sound and gestures with his other hand, at something falling out of the sky and into his lap – 'she was a gift, from heaven, landing out of the sky from nowhere. She was my, what did they call it when they made such a fuss after the war, my UFO, my unidentified flying object. We do not ask who sent you, where you are from, what you are. It is enough that you are here.'

He closes his eyes. I have exhausted him. To one side I can see the tall young woman with the clipboard, looking over at us, anxiously.

'Mr. Kowalski, it's not important, but I want you to know that your paintings have my blessing. My mother – she would be honoured. Thank you.'

I squeeze his hand one last time, disengage myself from his grip, and walk steadily out of the room, down the stairs and out into the cold Sheffield air.

Out of Reach

'Ist dies etwa der Tod?' (*'Is this perhaps death?'*)
[From 'Im Abendrot' ('At Sunset')
by Josef Karl Von Eichendorff]

'The word remains stubbornly out of reach. Not like something you stretch for at the back of the top shelf of a tall cupboard, where at least you can rest your fingertips on it. More like a bird that flits away into the undergrowth every time you make a move towards it. Always there, on the edge of your vision, but always disappearing before you can lay hands on it.'

Tom wrote that, nearly ten years ago now. It was when he first got frightened, and wanted to put down in writing what it felt like to have his world, the writer's world of words, slip away in the unsteady atrophy of his condition. Now, we struggle together, he and I – he with language, I with anger. I'm angry at this disease, eating away at him in front of me. I'm angry at him, for messing up my life. I'm angry at life, which was never meant to be like this.

He shuffles into the room, incompetently dressed, making the low moaning noise of a badly oiled piece of machinery about to grind to a halt. He takes a pile of papers from the kitchen work surface, brings them over to the table, and sits opposite me. With trembling fingers he transfers the papers across from one pile on his right to make another on his left, lifting each one with seeming concentration, looking at it briefly with the absence of comprehension that might signify that it's written in a foreign tongue, before putting it shakily down in its new place. At the end of the process he pushes the whole pile carefully across the table in front of him from left to right, before beginning again, methodically, painstakingly, in the same manner. All the while there's this low, tuneless moan, grating, nagging. I can feel the tide rising inside me, concentrate on my breathing, but I know I'm going to lose control even before it happens. As he starts the third cycle my coffee cup smashes down on the table top, sending liquid splashing across the table, the papers, his clothes.

'Stop it! Stop it! Just sodding stop it, for God's sake!'

I'm screaming at him, fists clenched, and he looks up with bewilderment, eyes wide with uncertainty and fear. He's going to cry. I know it. He's going to cry, and I can't bear this sense of child-like incomprehension. I rush round the table, kneel and pull him close to me, my kisses and tears and his tears and snot all mixed together. He isn't moaning now, and he strokes the back of my head and makes a kind of 'shushing' sound. I lean back, searching his face for meaning, but the eyes are blank. Whatever is inside there, it's out of reach to me. Maybe the comforting behaviour is just a kind of reflex, without significance. At least he's stopped crying.

'Here. Let's put your music on. You'll like that.'

I stand, scroll through the options on my phone and press play. After a moment's cueing, the slow undulation of the strings pours softly from the speakers, and there's that sudden shock that always hits me as I hear my own voice pick up the story of *Spring*, where Hesse's poetry is matched by Strauss's yearning, unspooling melody in dreams of love and longing. I turn away to the window, biting the side of my hand to hold back the tears. Why he had to fix on the *Four Last Songs* I'll never know, but these are all that's left that will reach him. He sits still, hands folded in his lap. He's entranced. I don't know on what level any of this means anything to him any more, but he's arrested, absorbed by the river of sound, elegiac, serene, content. Even the sudden flood of orchestral forces at the start of *At Sunset* doesn't shake him out of his trance, and as the flutes and solo violin trace their patterns across the darkening night sky at the song's close, he is rapt.

As for me, the exquisite familiar torture plays its own melody deep in the core of my being. This music was where the story of our lives ended and began again, charting its new and inevitable course all the way to here and now. Love, longing, loss.

*

My friend Jenny picked up the call moments after we'd started the afternoon rehearsal. I'd had a couple of meetings beforehand with the Maestro, and we'd run through the songs with a repetiteur the previous afternoon to iron out matters of tempo and phrasing. I'd waited for this moment, my debut with the orchestra at the Royal Festival Hall, for years. I'd done three or four Strauss operas, including an *Arabella* at the Met that gained pretty excitable reviews on its release on disc, but this was my first step in broadening my repertoire from opera to orchestral songs and lieder. We were only about twenty bars into *Spring* and I could see her pacing urgently up and down the aisle, wanting to catch my eye but not daring to interrupt an orchestra in full flow. Eventually the conductor stopped to have a word with the woodwind about balance as they took over the song's momentum at the end of the first stanza, and Jenny pushed forward, shaking, panicked.

'Sal. I'm so sorry. You need to come, now. Tom's been taken to hospital. He's had a fall, and, well, you need to come.'

It probably took moments only – an unscheduled break for the orchestra, hurried discussions with conductor and orchestral management team, a call to the hospital – before it was agreed that I'd stand down from the evening's performance. I knew there were always contingencies. I'd had the same sort of call myself from my agent ('How would you like to sing Susanna in *Figaro*? When? Oh, tomorrow. Milan. Good – because I've already booked your flights') so I knew that within minutes there'd be inserts printed for the evening's programme: 'Sally Henderson is sadly indisposed. In tonight's performance of Strauss's *Four Last Songs* and at very short notice we are extremely grateful ...' and so on.

In the car I finally got through to Tom. His voice was slurred, the words mouthfuls of syllables he was chewing on.

'Tom! You bastard! You're drunk, aren't you? Today of all days, you had to get pissed and fall over and ruin it all. You little shit, you.' I smashed the phone against the dashboard in front of me. Disappointment, anger, frustration, welling up in tears that I couldn't hold back.

Jenny took the phone from me, expertly pulled the car in to the side of the road, and took my hands in hers.

'Sal. Stop it. It isn't like that. He's had like a ... a stroke or something. I don't know. Wait till we get there. But it's not his fault.'

And it wasn't. There were physical tests, checking reactions, balance, hearing, eyesight, a CT scan, then a full MRI scan of his head and neck, and in the days that followed a stream of medical professionals, experts of one sort and another. We sat together, holding hands, as the consultant flicked through the images on the screen, highlighting the clustering of darker patches across the brain – 'think of it like little holes in a Swiss cheese', he said, not at all encouragingly – each a kind of mini-stroke, a point where the lights went out, the circuitry died, and the brain struggled to compensate. I asked the questions as though I were talking about someone else in a different life – 'Will his brain find ways round this? Is he going to get worse? What will happen to him?' – but the answers were hedged, reluctant.

*

Now, as I let myself back into the house, I know what has to happen. In the kitchen I can hear Jenny tidying up, and out in the garden the sound of *September* sweeps in doomed consolation from the speakers that Jenny has rigged up on the patio so that Tom can listen to his music and enjoy the afternoon sun. It's my recording again, I notice. I don't know if Tom can recognise my singing voice as mine any more, or whether this is just the version that the algorithms offer up on the basis of previous history, but I have to stop in the hallway and choke back the tears. *September* has always seemed the saddest of the songs to me – the garden in mourning, summer shivering in its dying domain, the longing for peace, and darkness, and sleep that death brings – and it's painfully apt.

I can't do this any more. The last five years of looking after Tom, the pause that I know is really the end of my top level singing career, have worn me down. I love him – how can I not love this man whose joys and sorrows are so closely woven in with my own, from that time way back when we were the golden couple of the British arts world, when, in the gushing words of a profile of the time in *The Observer*, we had the world at our feet. I look at my recordings on the CD rack, and at Tom's novels on the bookshelf, and I know that something precious of us will endure – even if the title of Tom's last novel, *Forgetting*, seems cruelly fitting, and his silence since it was published can no longer be put down simply to writer's block. But where now is the Tom that I knew? Not, truthfully, out there in the garden, sweeping up leaves as the autumnal glow of Strauss's music swells and fades.

It's not that I'm leaving him. I'm not just – in those awful words – 'putting him in a home'. But he needs more support than I can give, and, now all the preparatory visits and interviews and trial short-term stays are over, we have one more night.

It's a fine evening. I suggest a trip out in the car, which he likes – familiar novelty. We drive out onto the Downs, park up overlooking the valley where, years ago, we walked and flirted and started out on this journey. Does he recognise it? I don't know, though I chatter on about these memories, to stop the tears as much as anything else. Then he begins to get restless, and I resort one last time to Strauss, plug my phone lead into the car stereo's USB socket, and we listen again, from the oddly hopeless optimism of *Spring*, to the dying fall of *September*, to the rather desolate comfort of *Going to Sleep*, and then finally, with perfect timing, to *At Sunset*. I've never really trusted this song, with the flutes playing its conveniently situated larks, and the surely too contrived snatch of *Death and Transfiguration* on the horn, willing us to think that death is not the end. But this evening, as the darkness fills the valley below us, it's inevitable that up there, in the fading gloom, two birds thread their delicate tracery. Tom stirs, and points.

'Bir,' he says, and then again, 'Bir.' And then he says, or I so dearly want to believe he says, 'Love.' Then he's silent, though his eyes strain and his finger points, as the birds disappear, slowly blending into the dark, until it claims them, as it will claim us all.

Tom's finger continues to point, but in the silence at the song's close the birds are gone.

Out of reach.
Out of sight.
Out of mind.

*Inspired by the fragile beauty of 'Four Last Songs'
by Richard Strauss.*

Green Shoots

Rachmaninov's Symphony No 1 was first performed in March 1897, when he was 23 years old. The disastrous performance and scathing reviews provoked a lengthy depression and composing 'block' that lasted nearly three years. Eventually, he sought help from the hypnotherapist Dr. Nikolai Dahl, in daily sessions which lasted from January to April 1900. Whatever happened in those sessions, Rachmaninov pronounced himself 'cured', and dedicated his Piano Concerto No. 2 to Dr. Dahl. Several decades later, Rachmaninov's grandson claimed in an interview that all the fuss about Dr. Dahl was beside the point, and that what caused Rachmaninov to keep going back to see Dr. Dahl was the existence of Dahl's beautiful daughter. The problem with this account is that there is no evidence that Dahl ever had a daughter. But if she had existed….

*

Before the concert Sergei Vasilyevich comes into our box. He's bearing gifts. My father stands and grasps him by the hand, wishing him well. Sergei offers him a wrapped box, complete with ribbons.

'Should I open it?' father asks.

Sergei nods. Inside is an ornately bound copy of the score.

'The first page,' says Sergei. There is, almost, a smile.

I peer over father's shoulder, and there it is, at the head of the score. There, above the heading 'Second Concerto', is the dedication: 'A Monsieur N Dahl'.

My father wipes away a tear.

'Sergei Vasilyevich, it is an honour I do not deserve,' he says, his voice choked with emotion. 'I have treated many great figures in the arts over the years – Chaliapin, Stanislavsky, even the great Tolstoy himself has spent time in my study – and nobody has thought to dedicate a work to me. It is,' he says, reaching for his pocket handkerchief, 'it is an honour, Monsieur.'

Sergei looks down at my father. I am conscious yet again of the disparity in height, though Sergei would tower over almost everyone of my acquaintance.

'It is nothing but the truth,' he says. 'Before you, I could write nothing. And now...' He sweeps his arms wide, as if to encompass this new-found breadth of his imagination.

He turns to me. The almost smile is still there. He presents me with a package, in which, I discover later, is a book, a reference tome on orchids published only this year to great acclaim here in Moscow. He takes one of my hands in his enormous grip, rests his other hand on top of it.

'Green shoots,' he says. 'Tonight you will hear. Green shoots.'

*

Our first meeting, to be frank, was not promising. He closed the door to my father's study with a sigh that seemed to betoken relief. He stood for a moment in the lobby, as if unable to find the will to walk the short distance to the cloakroom where Anton would have helped him into his heavy coat and hat, and the cloak to keep out the biting Moscow winter. I was passing, carrying a jug of water through to the conservatory to continue my regime of feeding and watering.

My first impression? Tall, gloomy, rather lugubrious in expression, unsmiling, with a heavily lined face and close-cropped hair. Had I seen him in different circumstances I might have hazarded a guess that he was a convict, dressed in incongruous formal attire for the occasion. So many judgments, for better or worse, are made in the split second when we see someone for the first time. Another of my father's patients, I thought to myself; a hopeless case, no doubt.

My movement caused him to turn, and in that moment I saw the effort involved in trying to break free of the air of gloom enveloping him. He attempted a bow, and a smile so fleeting that had I not been paying attention I would have missed completely. He cleared his throat.

'Mademoiselle,' he said, holding out his hand as if to take mine in greeting. With both hands full, I shrugged helplessly. 'Here,' he said, 'allow me,' and before I could protest he relieved me of the jug of water. 'I will carry this for you,' he said. 'Show me where.'

I nodded further down the lobby area to the final door off to the right.

'In there,' I said. 'My conservatory.'

He set the jug down on one of the tiled areas next to my work bench and stood awkwardly, as though unsure of what should happen next. I held out my hand.

'Irina Dahl,' I said. 'And you are...'

'Forgive me,' he said. 'I forget my manners. Sergei Vasilyevich Rachmaninov.'

The name meant nothing then. But his mood, a kind of distracted preoccupation with something just out of sight, or perhaps something at the back of his mind, was familiar enough.

'Ah, you have been to see my father,' I said. 'Your first appointment?'

'Just so,' he said. 'I have been sent – that is, I chose to come – because I believe he may have the power to help me. At any event,' he said, the air of gloom returning in a wave, 'nothing else, it seems, can.'

An awkward silence followed. He seemed quite incapable of small talk.

'Well,' I said at length, looking around at the plants in my care, 'I have work to be getting on with here. If you will be seeing my father regularly we will no doubt meet again.'

'Every day,' he said, as though he were engaged in some kind of act of penance. 'I shall be here every day, at about this time.'

'Well,' I said, 'there will be other occasions to get to know each other, I am sure.'

He bowed, and took his leave. A cold fish, I thought. A cold fish.

*

My father's work, I should point out, is strictly illegal. Not, fortunately, that anyone is likely to stop him. It's just that officialdom here in Tsarist Russia has a fear of hypnotherapy as a practice, as though it might infect the populace with a kind of hysteria, or unlock forces of social disorder. But since he returned from training in France we have seen a steady stream of patients, or 'guests' as we describe them if anyone asks, finding their way to my father's study. I had no reason to think that Sergei Vasilyevich Rachmaninov would be any different to any of the others, who come and go, sometimes at the oddest hours of the day and night, to talk, or to be talked at, until their treatment is deemed to be at an end.

They do not usually pay attention to me. Perhaps they are too locked into their own closed worlds to observe the environment around them. Perhaps, as I walk around the house with my plants, appearing from and disappearing into my conservatory, they think I am merely one of the servants, and therefore officially beneath their notice.

I must confess, in case it strikes you as odd, that I paid more than usual attention to Sergei Vasilyevich. He carried with him an air of brooding melancholy, but there were glimpses of another man entirely that briefly, momentarily, broke the surface of his morose politeness. I made it my business to enquire after him. I found that I knew not him, but a fragment of his music, already. My father plays the viola well, and the piano passably, and there was a phase when he struggled with a piano piece until, eventually, he gave up and set it aside. But its sombre rise and fall melody, its syncopated rhythms, the agitated central section and huge climax, made it stick in my mind, and one day I had asked my father what it was he was trying to play, and he showed me the score: *Prelude in C# minor, Op.3 no.2*. The composer's name meant nothing to me at the time. But once Sergei Vasilyevich became encamped in my father's study every morning, it made me wonder about the imagination of a man who could write such a piece.

*

One morning, about a week or so after his treatment had started, I happened to be passing my father's study – I may have passed more slowly than usual, or listened more carefully to the voices from within – and I could hear my father's usual calmness-inducing tones. I knew from previous patients that his favoured method was to find the key to unlock the motivation of the recipients of his technique, and then focus, repeatedly, almost relentlessly, on that issue. His voice was calm, patient, measured. I could not catch it all – I may perhaps have put my ear to the door from time to time – but I heard enough.

'You will begin to write your next concerto,' my father's voice intoned soothingly. 'You will work with great felicity. It will be excellent.'

And on and on, seemingly round and round. From Sergei Vasilyevich himself, at that point, there came not a sound. He may have been in a trance-like state. He may even – my father assured me that this happened from time to time – have been asleep. But it gave me enough to make it imperative that I should be walking past the study door at precisely the point when I knew these sessions were scheduled to come to an end.

The fortuitousness of the coincidence of meeting having been thus acknowledged, I took it upon myself to offer Sergei Vasilyevich a tour of my conservatory. He followed, hands clasped behind his back, as I pointed out the fruits of my time and devotion. The effect on him, I was pleased to note, was encouraging. In truth, there are few collections of plants raised in such conditions, even in professional collections, that can rival mine in the whole of Russia.

The conservatory was a desolate place when my father returned from France and bought this apartment with its ground floor annexe which former owners had clearly at one time had a view to turning into a glasshouse. But apart from a few scrawny specimens the area had been completely neglected, the wood-burning stoves allowed to lie cold throughout the winter. It had, by the point at which I presented my work to Sergei Vasilyevich, been the product of five years' effort to bring the area to a state of such rich variety and profusion. You cannot, in truth, expect tender plants to survive a Russian winter, even indoors and cossetted to the extreme, without some ill-effects, but I could see that he was genuinely surprised by the richness and colour: bougainvillea and stephanotis climbed up to the roof beams and trailed across over our heads; in sturdy containers begonia and hibiscus still retained the odd fragrant flower. He nodded.

'You are, I see, a specialist in your field, quite as much as your distinguished father in his.'

His eyes took in the shades, textures, shapes, as though he had been standing in a gallery observing so many works of art. At last he turned to me.

'So many characters here. Like themes in a piece of music. The challenge is to wield them into a cohesive whole, or else all you have in noise and confusion. It makes, if I may say Mademoiselle, a positively symphonic whole.'

His eyes were alight at that moment. It felt as though something in his soul was stirring. I was, I must confess, moved by the reaction. He looked further, peering round into the various niches round the walls of my space.

At last, with an 'Aha!' of surprise, he turned and pointed to something. 'There, Irina, I see you have cultivated the perfect representation of me.'

I looked over to where he was pointing.

'Ah, my sad lemon tree,' I said. 'It is in mourning, is it not?'

He shrugged. 'It is surely dead.'

'Perhaps,' I said. 'I like to cultivate citrus fruit, and in the summer they can sit outside in their containers, in the sun trap in the corner of the garden over there. But they must be back indoors before the first frosts, and in late autumn we were, I confess, taken by surprise. As you can see, it is a mere skeleton, and it may well be that it will not revive, but I will nurture it, and wait and see.'

'It shall be the emblem of my condition,' he said. 'I have been accused of being as sour as a lemon from time to time by those who do not know me well. Perhaps,' he said, with what felt almost like flirtation, 'your lemon tree and I will both benefit from your nurturing.'

*

In the weeks that followed a routine was established. I no longer needed to loiter by my father's study to contrive an accidental meeting. Once his morning's hypnotherapy was at an end, Sergei Vasilyevich knocked politely at my conservatory door and joined me in the armchairs in which I sometimes paused to rest from the work I had been doing. Katerina brought coffee and biscuits from the kitchen and we sat and chatted like old friends. Sergei Vasilyevich got visibly younger, more alive. When I first saw him emerge from my father's study he could have been any age, stooped as if perhaps in his fifties or sixties, with the cares of depression weighing on his back and neck. Now I could see that beneath that shroud of gloom he was a young man – my enquiries indicated that he was a mere twenty-six, just two years older than me – and he stood more upright, shoulders relaxed, fingers no longer knotted together with tension.

I began to dress more carefully for these meetings. I would not have said that I wanted to appear more attractive, necessarily, but I found that I looked forward greatly to our conversations and I wanted to make a good impression. The truth, perhaps, is that I warmed to Sergei Vasilyevich the more he opened up about himself, and the more I knew about his life. He confessed to having felt insecure, that his grip on life was precarious, ever since his father's bankruptcy when he was merely ten years old, leading to the loss of the family estates and life in a cramped St. Petersburg apartment. The death of his younger sister the same year, and an older sister Yelena two years later only underscored the fragility of existence. The kindness of his paternal aunt and her daughters in giving him a place to stay here in Moscow as he grew from music student to full-time composer and performer had melted some of that emotional reticence but even so I could see he was easily discouraged by setbacks.

It took several conversations and much careful questioning on my part to uncover the cause of his writer's block for myself – I could, I suppose, have simply asked my father, but I knew that he did not discuss his patients outside the consultation room and in any case I began to consider Sergei Vasilyevich a good friend rather than a patient seeking treatment.

When he told me about the premiere of his first symphony, I confess I wept with him. He described slipping out of the concert hall, sitting on the stairs outside the auditorium and covering his ears with his hands to shut out the sounds. I would have been angry with the conductor for being drunk, but to Sergei Vasilyevich it was simply proof that he was a failure as a composer, and that his earlier successes counted for nothing. And the cruelty of the critics. How anyone could write such things – that these were like the sounds composed by students at a music conservatory in hell – was beyond what I could conceive. As he stood up to leave that day I confess I set aside convention and hugged him until the tears subsided for both of us.

At each visit he asked 'And how is my alter ego?', meaning the lemon tree. Through January and February it stood, skeletal and inert, as near to dead as made no difference. He looked at me with surprise.

'Why do you persevere?' he asked. 'You could dispose of it and simply get a new one. That's what I do when I meet setbacks in my music – I set the piece aside and turn to something else. At least, that's what I did until three years ago. Now, when I have composed merely one song, a melancholy thing called *Fate*, in these past eighteen months, I fear your lemon tree and I have more in common than you might hope.'

But in late March something astonishing happened. We had sat with our coffee and were making a tour of the conservatory before Sergei Vasilyevich took his leave. The lemon tree was our last port of call. And there, at a joint in one of the stick-like branches, was a tiny green shoot. We stared at it for some time, and it became clear that there was not just one fragile sign of life but three or four. Sergei Vasilyevich turned to me, took my hands in his, and kissed them passionately. His eyes shone.

'It is a sign,' he said. 'Look. It is coming back to life.'

He laughed then. It was the first time I ever heard him laugh – a low chuckle from deep inside his frame.

'Irina,' he said, looking at me with a renewed intensity, his hands still gripping mine, 'thank you. Thank you so much. You have revived me.'

I confess I thought he would kiss me then, and I held myself in anticipation of that moment. It never came. With one last squeeze of my hands, he turned, made the sign of the cross, and prepared to leave.

'I must see my cousin Natalya right away,' he said. 'I have so much to tell her.'

*

The Russian spring is a sudden, dramatic affair. One day there is snow and ice, a barren landscape. The next day the earth is shaken with such power you can literally hear the land cracking as the new season propels its way to the surface, the snow melting in torrents as the budding life force asserts itself unstoppably.

Within two weeks my father announced the news as we sat over our evening meal.

'You may know, my dear Irina, that I have been treating a young man these past three months, a fellow called Sergei Vasilyevich Rachmaninov. I must confess there were times when I despaired of ever effecting a change in him, but in these past few days I have noticed a profound difference in his demeanour. I truly believe something has shifted in him. Though I say it myself, my treatment has been a notable success.'

My father is a thoughtful man, and like so many thoughtful men he is almost entirely self-absorbed. He was wholly unaware of my conversations with Sergei Vasilyevich. I kept my counsel. But two weeks after that, my father pronounced the sessions with Sergei Vasilyevich at an end. He came to see me in my conservatory one final time. We admired the lemon tree with its urgent new growth and he told me, as one might share a shy confidence, that he had begun composing again, a piano concerto, and he had a theme for the slow movement already written, a theme born out of love and the renewal of life. I wept when he left.

*

The final chords of the concerto die away and the applause is overwhelming. Sergei Vasilyevich stands up from the piano, bows from the full height of his six feet six frame and proceeds from the platform. Naturally the audience will not let him leave without an encore, and, with a sense of inevitability, he plays the *C# minor Prelude*, its mournful tossing and turning heading straight for the listeners' hearts.

Afterwards we meet him backstage. There are handshakes, back-slaps, warm embraces from orchestral players and friends from his former days at the conservatory. Eventually the crowd thins and we have a brief word. There is more praise for the part my father has played in his recovery. He looks at me a little uncertainly. There is a pause. Eventually, he speaks.

'Monsieur Dahl, Irina,' he says, stepping back a little. 'I would like to introduce you to my fiancée. This is my cousin, Natalya Satina.'

A quietly smiling young woman of about my age stands before us.

'I have seen the transformation,' she is saying to us. 'I want to thank you – to thank both of you – for the support you have given to my dear Sergei. He is like a plant freshly in bloom.'

The blood rushes in my ears. I think I may faint, but somehow the stubborn perseverance I bring to my horticultural endeavours comes to my rescue. I manage a quick, 'How do you do? So pleased to meet you,' before there is something in my eye and I have to retire to the cloakroom to compose myself once more. A cousin? Surely he must know that the church will never consent to marry them – though I know there are ways round this for those sufficiently desperate. My heart feels gripped as by the first frosts of autumn, the green shoots of awakened longing cut off in their infancy. After a silent journey home, it takes many hours in the stillness of my conservatory before I feel ready for sleep to overtake me.

The Creative Impulse

This is a true story. Well, at the very least, this is as true as something can be that has the word 'story' attached to it. Perhaps I should just say, this is my story – or not, as you'll see. This is what happened to me, Phil Parker, writer of short stories. You can make your own minds up about it. Humans are story-making creatures, when all's said and done, so you'll probably have your own take on it. All I know is, sometimes the creative impulse takes you to some strange places. Let's face it, the human imagination is an odd thing, creating something where nothing existed before. Except that now, I'm more and more convinced by the opposite theory – that like the conservation of matter, the products of the imagination can neither be created nor destroyed, but only redistributed in different forms. As the man said, all those years ago, there is nothing new under the sun.

So, it's yesterday morning. I'm in my office. Nobody knows I'm here. Well, in the interests of accuracy, I should correct that: apart from Paula, to whom I've just sent a jokey text about taking up my chisel again to try to discover what's hiding inside this stubborn block of marble, and George down on reception, with whom my conversations, day to day, never vary – apart from these two, nobody knows I'm here.

The idea of renting a room in this shabby office building hadn't occurred to me until a few weeks back, when it presented itself as a creative solution to my latest bout of writer's block. Lots of creatives do it, said Paula over dinner. They treat writing like a nine-to-five job. Gets them out of the house, where there are so many distractions, and then there's nothing to stop the creative juices flowing. I've had this room for three weeks now, and for the first few days the effect was startling. I'd knock off 3000 words a day – good words, that is, not just any old stuff – and then head off home again, satisfied with my labours.

Recently, I confess, things have slowed up a bit. I spent a bit of time last week rearranging the rather spartan furniture to see if it might affect the creative alignment between my imagination and my surroundings, but it just served to confirm my prejudices about feng shui. Also, I realise I've brought a lot of my domestic habits to the office with me. I switch on my lap top, then check my emails, have a quick skim of the BBC website and *The Guardian*, fire off a few barbed comments to the 'Have Your Say' section below the political stories of the day, and by then, well, by then it's getting on for mid-morning and it's time for a coffee. So I wander downstairs, where, from behind his desk George says 'Coffee time?' on cue, and I nod and head off to Starbucks on the corner for a coffee and – don't tell! – the occasional pastry, and then I greet George again, and spend five minutes putting the world to rights. We'll have already done the weather and whatever sport was happening yesterday when I arrive first thing, so this mid-morning chat is more about man talk, the big issues of the day, politics or the economy or, if all else fails, last night's TV. Then it's back up three flights of stairs – the exercise is good for my heart, though the preceding pastry may or may not be good for either that or my creativity – and back to my desk.

Thing is, this story is a bit of a sod. You know sometimes how famous writers, when they're being interviewed on some prestigious arts programme, will say, 'I didn't choose this topic, you know. No, I feel as though this story chose me.' Well, it's never like that. This story chose me only in that I've got a title – in this case 'The Creative Impulse' – that I'm supposed to write to. God knows who chose that, but the read through is in a couple of days, so it's pretty much now or never. I'm stuck at about 700 words, and no matter what tricks I try, nothing more will come.

The outline has been in my head for weeks. It's about a sculptor, Elspeth. She's been making waves for a few years, starting to get commissions not just to decorate the glamorous glass-and-marble foyers of the offices of rich multinationals, but also for open spaces in city centres, the creative impulse in the service of the public good, and all that. She's drop dead gorgeous. That doesn't really matter, of course, but why choose to imagine someone who looks like the back of a bus? Actually, I suppose it does matter, because otherwise she wouldn't be having an affair with Keith Dolan, Associate Director at Tate Modern, and consequently she, and he, wouldn't find themselves being discussed by the cognoscenti of the arts world as the possible real-life models for the scandalous novel, *The Creative Impulse*, written as a *'roman a clef'* by Keith's embittered wife, the famous novelist Jacquie Dolan.

Are you keeping up with this? So, here is Elspeth, with her latest commission, and I know she's got this idea for a piece, 'The Destructive Impulse', in which she wants to show how the making of anything involves the destroying of something else. But how to give form to that idea? And how to make it not just about the petty, local experiences of Keith and Jacquie and her, but about Art, Art with a capital A, and Creativity, with a capital C? Come on, Elspeth, I think to myself. You can do this. Elspeth's problem is, let's face it, my problem. I can't finish the story until she's finished her art work.

'Come on, Elspeth,' I say. 'Help me. I need to know what you're going to do now. Tell me what it is.'

There's a knock at the door. This is odd. There has never been a knock at the door, all the time I've been here. Nobody – excepting Paula and George, that is – knows I'm here. I ignore it, concentrating hard on Elspeth and her stubborn block of marble, her – I make a little joke to myself – her creative block. There's another knock, more impatient this time.

'I'm not here,' I call out. 'There's nobody here.'

The door opens. The head, followed by the rest of the body, of – I cannot tell a lie – the most beautiful woman I've ever seen, appears, and moves towards me, hand outstretched.

'Phil?' she asks.

I nod, dumbstruck, offer my hand in return.

'Elspeth,' she says.

I can't tell you how long passes. She pulls up a chair and sits across the desk from me. I have no idea what's going on. I look down at my lap top, at the piles of notes on the desk in front of me, back at Elspeth again. I seem to have taken a vow of silence.

'Well?' she asks, composing herself. 'You wanted to talk to me.'

This is happening. This is really happening. This is happening to me, now. Elspeth, the sculptor (I can tell she's a sculptor because, drop dead gorgeous or not, her hands have the look of hands that do tough stuff for a living), Elspeth out of my story, is sitting across the desk from me.

It's probably a charade, I hazard a desperate guess. I've been set up. Maybe it's one of these 'reality TV' shows where people are tricked into believing something is happening to them. 'Smile – you're on Candid Camera' they used to say, when I was a kid. In a moment a film crew will come bustling in, and Paula, and there'll be laughs all round, and I'll have to pretend to having been fooled, and we'll all go out for drink. The more I try to imagine that, the more implausible it seems. Meanwhile, there's this woman sitting opposite me, waiting, not very patiently.

'Look,' she says, 'I'm a busy woman. I've got a commission I'm working on. I need to be back in my studio before very long. Can I help you?'

I somehow rediscover the ability to speak.

'Elspeth?' I ask. 'You're Elspeth? Elspeth the sculptor – that's your stuff in the atrium at the BFI on the South Bank?'

She nods.

'Elspeth…' – and I struggle with this next bit – 'Elspeth who is in my story?'

She nods again, smiles.

'If you like,' she says, enigmatically.

'Shit,' I say, more to myself than anything. My brain is whirling. I look closely at my hands, try to see if they're trembling more than usual. A wild thought strikes me. I try adding an experimental sentence onto my story. I type, "For a moment, Elspeth looks round her cramped studio space, looking for the nearest hammer. Maybe destruction has to come first, she thinks."

I look up.

Elspeth – or whoever this is – is shaking her head and frowning.

'Oh, I don't think I'd do that,' she says. 'I got all that destructive stuff out of my system at art school. You have to think about marble as though it's butter, not some lump of rock.'

I swallow. This is madness. OK – so there's a woman in my office, pretending to be a character in my story, or I'm hallucinating that there's a woman in my office pretending to be a character in my story. But to every question, she knows the right answer – where she studied, who gave her her first big break, even, though she doesn't make eye contact at this point, about Keith Dolan and the not-very-coded plot of Jacquie Dolan's infamous novel. The only plausible explanation is that there was something in the coffee I bought this morning. I decide to humour her.

'OK,' I say. 'Look, Elspeth, or whoever you are. We both have the same problem here, don't we? You have a block of marble and the idea for a work called 'The Destructive Impulse'. I have a short story to write called 'The Creative Impulse'. I can't finish my story until I know what you do next. So what are you going to do?'

She smiles.

'You won't like this,' she says. 'I'm going to talk to Jacquie Dolan.'

'What?' I ask. 'You can't do that. You're shagging her husband. It'll be like war breaking out.'

'Oh, I don't think so,' she says. 'That is, if I may say so, a very male way of looking at things. Besides, she's here now. No time like the present.'

She looks across the room towards the door, which opens. It's Jacquie Dolan, obviously. There are things that surprise me – I hadn't expected her to be so tall – but I'm chastened by the realisation that I've put so much imaginative endeavour into creating the irresistible Elspeth that I've not really filled out the details of the other characters in my mind much at all.

The atmosphere is, at first, somewhat frosty. I sense that these are two cats testing the boundaries of each other's territory. Before I realise how stupid it sounds, I offer them both a drink, and imagine myself heading down past George's desk, saying 'Oh, I'm just out to buy a couple of chai lattes for my two principal characters.' Yes, that would work. Fortunately – maybe you can do this in fiction – Jacquie has a couple of shot glasses and a miniature bottle of vodka in her bag, and this seems to suit them fine. Eventually the subject of Keith comes up. I expect explosions, but Jacquie is cool, amused.

'After all,' she says, 'that book has made me a great deal of money.'

This is crazy. This isn't what's supposed to be happening in my story. As soon as there's a brief lull in their conversation I tap the desk, impatiently.

'Look, ladies,' I say. 'I'm glad to be the facilitator of this ever so touching reconciliation, and all that, but no. This can't happen. This is not in my story. This is not how it goes.'

They fix me with the sort of stare that brooks no argument.

'Oh, I think you'll find it is,' says Elspeth, in the sort of voice that my mother used to reserve for those moments when she'd been called into school to see the head teacher about my latest misdemeanour. I swallow hard, and try again.

'Look, who's in charge here? Whose story is this? Who is the author of this tale?'

For a moment, this brings the action to a halt. They look at each other, and Jacquie speaks.

'Let me – one writer to another – answer this, Elspeth dear.' She faces me directly. 'You are. Of course you are. The author is always in absolute and complete control.'

I sit back in my chair, affirmed, but she continues.

'But any author worth his, or her, salt, any author who knows their characters, knows their wishes have to be respected, that you can't force characters to behave a certain way or the reader will feel they're being dictated to.'

She holds her hands up, silencing my protests.

'Look,' she says, 'you need to speak to my dad about this,' and before I can stop her she's tapping a message into her mobile, and, this being fiction, before too long has elapsed there's another knock at the door, and a stocky, greying figure, with metal-rimmed glasses, a dog collar and a benevolent air, steps forward to greet me.

'The Reverend Anthony Trescothick,' he announces. 'You must be, ah...' – he appears to be consulting some sort of memory bank situated just over my left shoulder – 'You must be Mr. Parker, the writer. We've met before, I think.'

I can't help myself. I stare down at the sheets of A4 on my desk, shuffle through them searching in vain for any preliminary notes that might suggest that at one stage I contemplated giving Jacquie Dolan a vicar for a father. There's nothing.

'I don't think so,' I say, as evenly as possible. 'And now, if you don't mind...'

'Ah, I think you have,' he says. 'My church, St. Andrews, is just down the road. In fact, we said hello only this morning when you came out of Starbucks after your morning coffee. Remember?'

This is, again, madness. Yes I did, I did say hello to someone as they came down the steps of the local church. I didn't know he was Jacquie Dolan's father. Then I stop myself. Jacquie Dolan is a character in my story. St. Andrews presumably has a real life vicar, not just a fictional one thought up to suit the occasion.

But it's no use. As the afternoon wears on I sit and watch them as they discuss with each other on the other side of my desk. Rev. Trescothick, perhaps not surprisingly given his occupation, has some fairly firm views on what should happen in my story. Gradually they explore options. Will Elspeth move in with Keith? No, probably not – it will cause too much upset to too many people, and in any case she's not sure he really loves her.

'I'm not sure he really loves anyone other than himself,' says Jacquie, aside, as tactfully as she can, which isn't very tactfully at all.

Will Jacquie blow the lid on the background to her novel? Not yet, she says – at least, not until after the film version comes out. Will Elspeth carry on with her sculpture, and in what form? This goes on until I can take no more.

'Look – stop! Stop it right now! You are my characters. I'm in charge. I could write you out of it, completely. End of. See?'

The Rev. Trescothick waits for the air to still, puts his fingertips together as though in the beginnings of an act of prayer, and addresses me.

'Phil – if I may call you Phil, when we barely know each other. Phil, tell me, do you believe in God?'

'What?' I say, bewildered. 'What? What do you mean, do I believe –'

'Please,' he continues. 'Forgive me. There is a point to this. So, Phil, do you believe in God?'

I shuffle some bits of paper hesitantly in front of me. They can see I'm stalling.

'I'm not sure I could say one way or the other, but OK, well, yes, in theory.'

'Thank you,' he says, as though I've passed some first test. 'So, Phil, let us look at the world around us. All these people, going about their busy lives. All of us, with our various wants and needs, our hopes and fears, our moments of joy and despair –'

'Dad,' Jacquie quietly interjects. 'Not a sermon. OK?'

'Ah, yes. Yes. Sorry my dear.' He pats her arm benevolently. 'Daughters, eh?' he beams at me. 'You'll have one of your own one day. Just wait and see.'

The pause at that point is just a little longer than is good for any of us, so he proceeds.

'As I was saying. All these people. Exercising their free will, are they not? Not pulled one way or the other by a God who controls their every predestined move. Yes?'

I can see that this isn't the moment to get into a debate about creation, let alone free will and predestination, so I just nod.

'And there *you* are,' he continues. 'The God, if I may say so, of your own created world. You speak these characters into existence. Their world was without form and void, and you blessed them with the divine spark of your creativity.'

He looks again at Jacquie, notes her warning glare, and goes on.

'Yes. Not a sermon. So, Phil, these people you have created. Are they free? Can they choose? Surely they must, or they will never live at all.'

He sits back, beams another of those benevolent vicarly beams, and waits. There's a long pause.

'Yes. OK, OK, I accept. You can't force characters to do things or they won't be believable. But still, I'm in charge, remember. My story.'

The Rev. Trescothick leans his head acquiescently to one side.

'Just so, Phil, just so. But still, the question remains – what will they do? What will *we* do?'

I shrug. One thing I do know is that it's time for me to go home.

'A question for tomorrow, I think,' I say. 'I'll sleep on it.'

Trescothick looks across at the two women.

'We have some time,' he says. 'We could help you. You know, do some preliminary planning before you get in tomorrow. We could have a word with George and then let ourselves out.'

Resistance is pointless. I get my coat, and within seconds Jacquie has taken my place at the lap top and the three of them have their heads together in conference.

'Right,' I say, feeling like this must be some kind of dream. 'I'll be off then. I may see you tomorrow.' I try out a tentative smile but give up soon enough.

'Oh, I doubt that,' says Trescothick. 'We'll be gone long before that. I'm sure we won't trouble you again.'

I pull the door closed behind me, and for a moment I rest my head against it, listening. Their voices are urgent, engaged, increasingly confident. I wander downstairs, and feel constrained to add to my usual farewell to George.

'I've left some, er, some colleagues of mine upstairs in my office. They'll check out with you before your shift is ended.'

'Right you are, Mr. Parker. See you tomorrow.'

'Good night, George. See you tomorrow.'

The slow walk home does me some good, the bottle of red over dinner even more good, and I sleep deeply, and wake as though the story has sorted itself in my mind without me really having had to think about it. The walk to the office this morning is brisk, optimistic.

'Morning, George. Lovely day again, I see,' I say.

The usual formula. I start to make my way across the foyer towards the stairs. George looks up from his desk, frowning. He half rises from his chair.

'I'm sorry, sir. Can I help you?'

'Just saying what a lovely day it is,' I say again. 'I'll head on up right away, I think. It's going to be a good writing day. I can feel it in my bones.'

'I'm sorry, sir.'

He's apologetic, but firm. He consults the papers on his desk.

'Who is it you want to see? I'm not sure there are many people in this early, but I can ring for you. And your name is?'

'George, come off it.' There's a laugh behind my words, but a rising tide of panic too. 'It's me, Phil. My office is on the third floor. I'm writing the Great British Short Story, remember?'

He gives me the sort of look that makes me think he's trying to humour me. He makes a great play of consulting his lists.

'I'm sorry, sir. There's nobody who has a room on the third floor, at least nobody called Phil. What did you say your surname was?'

'Look George, stop it. It's me, Phil, Phil Parker. We talk every morning about the weather and the footy. Remember? It's me, me.'

I can see by the look in his eyes that he's contemplating calling security, so I try not to make a fuss.

'George, humour me, ok? Come with me to the third floor. I'll show you my office. I can describe its interior for you now, ok, so we'll both know it's full of my stuff. Come on. I'll prove it.'

I can see George mulling this over in his jobsworth mind.

'Well, sir, this is highly irregular. Highly irregular indeed. But ok, just this once.'

He locks everything away behind his desk, then leads the way up the three familiar flights of stairs, and we stand outside the familiar battered, plain office door. He juggles with the mass of keys on his various chains and unlocks the door.

'You can have a quick look inside, sir,' he says, by way of warning, 'but then I'm afraid I must ask you to leave.'

I look at him as though one of us has taken leave of our senses, and then follow him through the open door.

Inside the room is just as I described it to him. Well, almost. It's tidier than usual – they must have straightened things out a bit before they left. My eyes skim the filing cabinet, the worn wooden chairs, the desk – and there on the desk is a manuscript. A finished manuscript. It's hard to read upside down and from halfway across the room, but I can just about make out the title on the front page: 'The Creative Impulse' by...

'I'm sorry sir,' says George. 'You really need to go now. The gentleman who has this room will be in very soon.'

And that's it. I'm down the stairs, across the foyer and out onto the street before it occurs to me what has happened. Creative impulse or not, like God before me, it appears that I've been written out of my own story.

Mistaken

Here again, I see. Always in the same places. Just sitting. One of them – the one with a face like a slapped arse – with her nose in a book most of the time, or jabbing away at something in her hand. The other one, with the nice eyes, she keeps looking at me. As if she's waiting for something to happen. Her hands reach out across the sheet and hold onto another hand. Sometimes I can feel it, and then that other hand must be mine. Mostly though I sit here, behind my eyes, and wait. Sometime, long ago, I remember the swimming baths. Who could sit on the bottom for the longest. Watching those thrashing legs, arms appearing and disappearing. And that long, muffled, roaring, booming noise of the water in my ears. Like that now, I think. Underwater. That's how it feels.

Sometimes I think I see them at the window, noses pressed against the glass. Their mouths open and shut, like they're shouting. They wave, and then I understand. Come and play. I watch them running round and round, or dashing in and out of a skipping rope, Connie holding one end and chanting a song about sweethearts and knickers, but then they wave from the branches of the trees along the edge of the green. Some of them fly up higher, and somehow they're birds, their wings waving goodbye. I want to run after them but everything is so heavy, nothing will move for me. If I focus really hard I can raise my hands, but the effort is like lifting that old suitcase just with my little finger. I close my eyes again, exhausted.

They're here again. I must have slept, I think. When I open my eyes, she's holding my hand. Her voice is a long way off, but I know it's her.

'Mum,' she's saying. 'Hello, Mum. How are you feeling?'

I wait to see what happens. If anyone will answer. It must be my turn, but when I open my mouth nothing comes out. She's smiling at me.

'Mum, it's me. Sophie. We've come to visit you again.'

She looks sideways. Slapped-arse woman looks up at me briefly from her book and then looks down again. All this feels like such an effort. She's talking some more. Her voice is nice, it feels like satin against my skin, but I just let it drift past. I'm not sure I know I've closed my eyes, but the voice slips away as though she's talking into a headwind. I may be mistaken, but I think she's my daughter.

When I open my eyes again, Connie is there. She's wearing that old pinafore dress she always had. She holds out her hands so I can see the strap marks.

'See, told you I wouldn't tell,' she says.

She makes me prick my finger and when she's done hers we push our fingertips together.

'Sisters in blood,' she says. 'Make no mistake, Alice. Sisters in blood. Always.'

Then she fades away, and I can see past the end of the bed to the blinds, swaying slowly in the breeze from the open window.

Some days I know where I am. There's a brisk young man in a shirt and tie who smiles at me as though he likes me and talks to me about my blood pressure and the need to keep an eye on my heart.

'Broken long ago,' I tell him, and he laughs, but not unkindly, I think.

If I peer out of my right eye I can see the drip hooked up to a stand by the bed, and I can follow the line down to the back of my hand, where it disappears into a dressing. This must be a hospital. I try to get out of bed, but the effort is like shifting furniture. I close my eyes instead, and watch what's going on behind them.

It's a ballroom. Well, a dance hall, maybe. I watch Connie sweep past, eyes flashing, on the arm of that serviceman of hers, Tommy Johnson. He grins at her, and when they go past a second time, he grins at me, too. He has such nice eyes. It makes me feel tingling, wanted somehow. Then Frank takes my hand and we join them on the floor, swaying to the music, and he puts his hand on my back and lets it slide down to the base of my spine, where it rests, warm and alive. I don't know about Frank, but he likes me, and that seems to be enough. After the dance we sit down, but now he's wearing a suit and I seem to have my wedding dress on, and everyone is smiling at us and there's a man somewhere with a flash camera. Frank grins at me.

'Mr. and Mrs. Dobson, eh?' he's saying.

I might be mistaken, but I think he's my husband.

Some days a lady comes with some food. 'Coloured,' I'd have called her once, but I don't think I'm allowed to say that any more.

'Eat it all up, Alice dearie,' she says to me, offering me spoonfuls with a smile.

I get all this mixed up with feeding Sophie when she was little, so sometimes I expect her to end up eating it, not me.

'Nice bit of ice cream for afters?' she asks, as though I were a child again. Perhaps I am. I close my eyes again and she goes away. Later the ice cream is just a pool, listlessly white in the bottom of the plastic bowl.

Later that day, or perhaps it's another day, I open my eyes with a shock. At the foot of the bed is Tommy, naked as the day he was born and standing to attention, just for me.

'Tommy,' I gasp. 'What's all this? What if someone sees us?'

He gives me that smile again, his eyes soft and caressing.

'Thought you must be lonely,' he says, 'what with Frank being away at sea and all.'

He starts to make his way round the bed.

'What about Connie?' I ask him. Sisters in blood after all.

'She's at her mother's,' he says, matter-of-factly. 'Our secret, this.'

I try to push him away, but we know I'm only pretending, and he slips underneath the covers and before I know it he's eased me out of my nightdress. He talks to me all the time, and when he does it to me it's not rough like Frank but rocking gently like we're the ones at sea until I cry out at the pleasure of it, and the nurse comes back and says, 'Are you all right, Mrs. Dobson? Is there anything you need?' and for a long time I don't know where I am or what has happened to me at all. I have a vague sense of being embarrassed, as though I might have done something I shouldn't.

Time passes. It must do, I suppose, because I can watch the shadows slide across the room and end up on the other side of my bed by the door. Sometimes Sophie is there, with the slapped-arse woman. Sometimes she's just on her own.

'Val has to be in work today,' she says, by way of explanation.

I don't know about Val. I can't remember Sophie having a friend called Val as a child, but I can't remember much about Sophie not being a child, and she's definitely not a child now.

'You remember Val, don't you?' she asks me once, when my eyes must show that I don't. 'You were at our civil ceremony. Look.'

She shows me some pictures on a little screen she has. Sophie and slapped-arse woman holding hands and kissing. And there's one of me standing beside them, looking a bit lost and out of place, to be honest. It must have happened, but I can't remember, though it's not the sort of thing you'd be mistaken about, is it, not with all that dressing up and ceremony.

'Where's your husband?' I ask, wondering.

'Oh, Mum,' she says, in a voice that sounds like I'm a disappointment to her. But she holds my hand and tries not to let me see the tear that slips down her cheek. I might be mistaken, but I think she loves me.

There are days when nothing seems to happen at all, not in the hospital room and not behind my eyes, either. Blank, both of them. Or I'm aware of people – nurses I suppose, or whatever they call them these days, nursing assistants or something – doing things to me, turning me over or washing me or tutting over me, or sometimes just talking over me to each other as though I were some artefact they were preparing to put on display. I let it all happen to me, or to someone else.

One day I feel that Connie is there. She's angry and sad at the same time. I know there's something I'm not supposed to say, or do, but I can't remember what it is.

'Look at you,' she says, eyes flashing. 'Don't think I don't know what you're like. Shame on you! And I thought we were sisters in blood, too.'

I try to put my hand over my stomach, involuntarily, to disguise the change in me.

'Connie, I didn't –' I say, but I did. I know I did.

I close my eyes, hope that Connie will go away and the nice, kind nurse will come back to bring me ice cream, but she doesn't.

'We're finished,' she says to me, in a voice that sounds like a slap. 'Me and Tommy are going away, and we're not coming back. If you so much as ever try to get in touch with either of us again, I'll swing for you, make no mistake, see if I don't.'

When I open my eyes, she's gone, though when I carefully bring my free hand up to my face I can feel the tears. My heart beats faster. What would the nice young man in the tie think if he saw me in this state? I run my hand down and over my belly. The swelling has gone, and I want to shout back to Connie, 'Look. Come back. Look, I'm not pregnant after all,' but it's too late, in all senses. Connie has gone. And Sophie is here. Proof, and no mistake.

'What is it, Mum?' she asks. 'You've been crying. What's wrong?'

I don't think I have the words for this.

'Your father,' I say, as though to be honest now is better than all those years of pretence.

'Mum,' she says, gently, 'Frank died a long time ago. You remember.'

It's too hard, and I'm too tired. I lie still, holding her hand, until sleep claims me again.

Other people come and go. Some of them are real. Others I'm not sure about. There's a consultant and a cluster of young men and women with him, like a mother duck with a straggle of chicks just about keeping up. He looks at me, just the once, but I'm a condition, a diagnosis and a treatment, though I get the sense that there isn't any, or at least nothing that will work for a broken heart. There are nurses. There's a hospital porter who wheels my bed along a corridor, down in a lift and out into another room full of bleeping noises and hushed whispers in the darkness.

'We're just doing a few tests to check how your heart's responding,' a young woman shouts, as though I were a great distance off. Then the porter wheels me back, sets the bed in place in the same room as before, and bows with a flourish.

'It's been a pleasure, ma'am,' he says, with a wink just like Tommy used to do.

Then maybe this picture isn't real, but Sophie comes one day with an old lady and says, 'Mum, look, it's Connie. You remember Connie, don't you? I found her on Facebook and told her you were in here and that, well, that she might want to see you.'

I stare, at least as much as it's polite to stare, to make sure it's really her. It seems to be, even though she's much older than I remember. I don't have much to say – it all seems too much effort, and in any case what could I say that wouldn't make Sophie upset in the end.

Sophie keeps turning to her and saying, 'It's the medication, you know. They have to keep her sedated.'

But as she gets up to go, Connie leans over so I can see and takes my free hand in hers, pushing our fingertips together.

'Sisters in blood,' she whispers.

Then she's gone, and Sophie too, and the room seems especially cool and still. I watch the shadows slip along the wall some more until they almost reach the door. Sometimes it opens – someone coming to check on me, 'doing my obs', they call it – but I lie still with my eyes closed until they've gone again. I don't want to be disturbed. Not just now. I concentrate really hard. Yes. If I'm not mistaken, there's Tommy at the foot of the bed, naked as the day he was born, but standing to attention, just for me.

A Noise in the Night

The instant you wake, a wave of adrenalin courses through you, an aftershock of horror. A second or two later come the doubts. Surely it couldn't have happened? But feeling round under the duvet you find your phone, usually kept on your bedside table, and the picture of pulling it close to you, out of sight, is as vivid as it was in the darkness earlier. Slowly, you sort through the snapshots of memory in your head – the sudden jolt of wakefulness, the familiar sound of the door key turning in the lock, the not-quite-creak of the back door opening. That's when you grabbed the phone and held it close, like a charm, like a weapon, listening for more than the blood pounding in your ears. Then silence. No footsteps on the stairs, no pushing against the bedroom door. Nothing. And so you'd drifted off into an uneasy sleep, populated by shadowy threats.

And oddly, or at least it seems so now, the sense of him, or someone, or something, slipping under the duvet behind you, holding you close, two spoons cupped together, comforting. The sensation is so intense that you reach back behind you, expecting his presence, but there's nothing, just the aching distance of empty sheet stretching away. Six weeks on and you still expect to see him, though you know death is final and the house is empty apart from the noisy rattling sounds you make to prove to yourself that you're still really there.

Dressed, you make your way downstairs. The kitchen is empty, everything as it was except – you clutch your throat to stifle the scream – except that by the sink is an empty glass, empty except for the dregs of milk that he always used to leave after breakfast.

'Roy?' you ask the empty air. 'Roy? Is that you? Are you there?'

You sit abruptly, the kitchen chair pulled back against the wall so nothing is out of sight. Idiot, you think. Stop it, idiot, get a grip, simple explanation, must be, he's dead, he's not coming back, he's certainly not leaving you messages in a used glass of milk. Is he. Is he? Before you can stop them, the sobs rake through you, the loss, the rage, the sheer outrageous disbelief that he might go, simply go away and leave you.

The morning passes slowly. Breakfast, a bit of television, a bit of hapless tidying, though you eye the dirty glass by the sink warily and can't bring yourself to wash it up or put it in the dishwasher. You wonder about phoning Alice, though what would you say? Can you come round for a bit – just in case Roy puts in an appearance six weeks after the funeral? You make yourself go out and do a bit of shopping, though you've had no appetite ever since. Back home, as you turn the key in the lock and push the door open you hear the TV in the front room, and the smell of cooked food wafting from the kitchen. You want to shout out a greeting but nothing comes but a croak. You blunder through the hallway and push open the front room door.

He's there. In his usual armchair, news channel muttering to itself in the background. He looks up.

'Oh hello, love. Wondered where you'd got to. Made myself a bit of lunch, hope you don't mind that I didn't wait, but there's stuff to do.'

Sounds fail to form themselves into words. You hold your shopping bag – a loaf, a plastic bottle of milk, a packet of biscuits – under your chin, a token shield against the unknown, the unknowable. He seems not to notice that you might have been turned to stone.

'Well, best be off. Busy afternoon. Seeing Don in the club later, but I'll be back before dinner.'

He picks up his jacket, feels inside it for his keys, phone, wallet, and is gone.

You have no idea how much time passes, until suddenly the thought strikes with the certainty of doom. He was at the club with Don when he – when he –. You dash for the front door, stumble down the path to the gate, shouting.

'Roy! Roy! Come back! Roy!'

He is nowhere to be seen.

*

Weeks pass. Life resumes its slow, numbing routine. No sign of Roy. You haven't told anyone about his appearance. What would be the point? Nobody would believe you, not even Agnes, and she claims to believe in all sorts of crazy stuff. Each day is like sleepwalking, where the effort to eat, to dress, to stop the place from falling into disorder, comes from somewhere beyond you and seems to have nothing to do with the numbness that forms a screen between you and the outside world.

The girls have been great, you know that. Taking you out when you're not brilliant company, trailing in front of you visits to the cinema, the gym, the odd stately home, like so much bait to entice you back into the world. They dispense wisdom with the casseroles and cakes they bring round, as though feeding you up on some kind of life regime.

Weeks become months. Talk of Roy drops casually into conversations without being accompanied by waves of grief or panic or anger. He is in the past tense. Your friends curate his memory, carefully, like a tender bloom, whilst avoiding hagiography. Roy was, you know, no saint. It was a fragile marriage that often came apart at the seams. He left more than once – not, you want to think, for another woman, but just because life together was unbearable. But he always came back, quiet, chastened, ready for another go.

There are dates best avoided. Christmas and New Year you spend with your sister and her family in Hull, haunting the family meals and the frosty walks in the Wolds like a visitor from another world, tolerated, muffled in cotton wool and fed, always fed, as though carbohydrates are a cure for all life's ills, and death's too. And now it's your wedding anniversary. Alice and Agnes take you out for the day, offer to spend the night, but you decline. It'll be fine. Wedding anniversaries were never a big deal anyway.

You're in bed before midnight and drifting off well before the shipping forecast. Then – no warning – there's a rapping on the glass of the back door. You peer at your phone. 12.30am. Nobody knocks at your door at that time. Maybe it's from next door. Maybe the baby's ill or something. And again – rapping, more urgent this time, continuous, demanding. You wrap yourself carefully in your dressing gown, take your phone with you, and head downstairs. Without an outside light it's not obvious who might be there, so you go right up to the glass before switching on the kitchen light.

The world slips a little on its axis. It's him. Roy, standing there in the rain, holding an inadequate umbrella and a large bouquet of flowers. You know it can't be, but it is. It takes considerable effort not to scream, but you watch your hand as it takes off the newly-fitted chain and turns the key in the lock. You open the door, buffeted by gusts of cold, damp air. He stands there, waiting. You can't find any words, so you wait, too. Finally, he makes the first move.

'Can I – can I come in?' he asks.

You step back a little, a wordless shrug, hand still on the key in the lock. He eases past you, shoes squelching on the laminate floor, little pools forming in his wake. He puts the umbrella down carefully, straightens up and holds out the roses.

'Here,' he says. 'For you. For our anniversary. Didn't want you to think I'd forgotten.' There's a ghost of a smile, tentative, almost shy. 'It's twenty years, you know.'

No words arrive. When nothing makes sense, why should you worry about anything making even less sense. Twenty years? You're tempted to point out that you've been married, on and off, for thirty-one years when he – but you can't bring yourself to finish the thought. The autopilot kicks in.

'Tea?' you ask, filling the kettle. 'You must be soaked through.'

He sits at the kitchen table, looking round as though a little disoriented, as though it's not quite a familiar scene, and looks over to you. Odd – younger, less stooped, less balding. It doesn't seem worth questioning it. You busy yourself with the roses, arrange them in a vase and place it on the table, pour the tea and hand him a mug.

'No biscuits, I'm afraid. I've stopped buying them since you –'

You stop. Nothing you say will make sense. Fortunately, he has plenty of words.

'I've been thinking,' he says. 'About us. About how to go on. And I'd like to ask you if I can come back. Don't – don't rush to answer. Just think about it. I'm not asking you if I can stay now. I'll have my cuppa and go. But we're a team, you and me.' Half a smile, almost boyish. 'We belong together. We're good for each other. Well,' another boyish grin, 'most of the time.'

There's more, but you can't make sense of any of it. He talks, you listen, nod, wonder who this is talking to you, who you are listening to it all. He finishes his tea, gets to his feet, eases his way into his sodden coat and reaches inside a pocket for a damp piece of paper.

'Here,' he says, 'this is where I'm staying. Ring me when you've thought about it.'

He stands by the back door, takes your hand and raises it to his lips and kisses it.

'Goodnight, love,' he says, and pulls the door closed behind him.

You stand in a trance for minutes on end. Nothing makes sense, but the pools of water of the floor are real, and the dregs in the bottom of his cup, and the damp smell of his sweat, and the flowers. You lock up carefully, turn out the light and head upstairs to bed, where you sleep implausibly peacefully. In the morning you head downstairs, where a vase of roses awaits you on the kitchen table.

*

There are no easy ways of having that conversation. The girls treat you like you're stressed, or like grief has made you hallucinate. You point to the roses, the crumpled piece of paper with an illegible address on it, but as none of it makes sense even to you, it's asking a lot for it to make sense to anyone else. Eventually you stop trying, and life subsides into its familiar routines.

You realise with a shock that you've missed Roy's birthday, but nobody makes an appearance during the night, demanding to be let in. In fact, four days pass before you make the discovery. Alice and Agnes seem to regard it as a good sign, as proof that you're 'moving on', that you're finding your feet again. You might feel the same, were it not for the fact that Roy populates the fringes of your mind, like the memory of a lost wisdom tooth. You can't tell the girls this, but you know Roy will be back, eventually.

Sooner rather than later, as it happens. Your birthday is nothing special – nobody celebrates being sixty-two – but the girls insist on throwing a party in your back garden, and there's music and dancing until nearly midnight, when you promised the young couple next door and their baby girl everything would be shut down for the night. You wave everyone off, as they meander down the street in the dark, and then you go back down to the garden to switch off the lights dotted brightly about the flower beds, and take time to smell the honeysuckle's bloom by the back door.

The noise startles you, close behind you as you stare into the darkness. You spin round – and there he is, putting down his briefcase with a thump and letting his overnight bag rest against it. He reaches inside it for something indistinct and steps closer.

'Here,' he says, holding out a card. 'Told you I'd get back if I could. The flights were all on time for once. Happy birthday, sweetheart.'

You slip a finger underneath the flap of the envelope and pull out the card. The blood roars again in your ears. It's like you might be drunk, but you know how much you've had so it can't be that. 'Happy 30th Birthday!' the card announces. You sit down on one of the garden chairs, a puppet with strings so slack you feel your strength is all gone. Roy seems not to notice, and the next thing you know he's kneeling before you and holding out a small box. You know what's in it without having to look.

'See,' he says, suddenly awkward, 'I brought you this. I wondered if, well, you know, you might like to marry me.'

The tsunami crushes the breath from your body. It's too much, too complicated, too utterly impossible to comprehend. You manage a strangulated sob, and throw your arms round his neck, his all-too-real younger adult's neck. Eventually you realise he's been talking all this time.

'You know, now we're both in our thirties, it's not like we're kids any more. I've got a proper job, and your training finishes next year, and, well, your folks have left you this house' – he gestures behind you – 'so it seems a shame not to have a family living in it.'

You manage to get through the next few minutes without saying yes, but without saying no either. Fortunately he doesn't want to stay the night – he's told his parents he'll be back as soon as his flight gets in – and you get away with a promise to give him an answer tomorrow.

You close all the doors and lock yourself in. Taking the 30th birthday card with you, you head upstairs to the spare room, to the box on top of the wardrobe with its thick layer of dust. You haven't looked inside for years, but you know what's there. Underneath the faded photos and the certificates for this and that are a batch of birthday cards you've kept for no reason at all, and there it is: 'Happy 30th Birthday!', a card from Roy, and inside it his illegible scrawl: 'Welcome to a new decade! Why not spend it with me, Mrs. Roy?' and an image of a face, winking.

You have no memory of falling asleep, and wake up on the floor of the spare room, back and hips aching, and still clutching two identical 30th birthday cards.

*

You know you aren't done with him yet. There has to be another encounter, at least one more. There's no point saying any of this to the girls, so you don't even try. They take your preoccupation, your distance, as just another step in the grieving process. Their acceptance is touching, even if they're no help. You stare at the calendar, thinking. There are no likely dates coming up – in the nearly 12 months since his death you've got through Christmas, and your wedding anniversary, his forgotten birthday and then yours. You wonder about the anniversary of his death, and whether that would be too predictable, too like fiction. Maybe there's some special date that you've forgotten, some moment on the calendar that means something to him. There's no telling.

You sleep badly, always listening, always alert for the noise the night that will signal his presence. Sometimes you wonder about leaving the doors unlocked so he can get in whenever he wants. But days pass, weeks, time stretching out before you in unpunctuated monotony.

It's a distant rattle at the window that pulls you back up from the depths of sleep. There it is again, a scattering of grapeshot, a squall of hailstones. When it comes the third time, you drag yourself from bed and stare out of the bedroom window. On the ground below a face peers up at you, waving, holding a finger to its lips. You open the window.

'What is it?' you ask. 'Who's there?'

'Sssshh!' he offers in a stage whisper. He points to the other back bedroom. 'Your folks!' he says, as though it's obvious.

You watch as he struggles with a ladder, leans it precariously against the wall by your bedroom window, and climbs gingerly towards you. Eventually you're more or less on a level with each other.

'Hi!' he stage whispers. 'It's me. Roy.'

'I know,' you say, even if it is and isn't the Roy you've lived your life with. He's so – well, so young.

'Look,' he says, urgently, as though afraid of being discovered at any moment. 'I'm off to uni in the morning, and, well, I didn't want to leave without saying goodbye to you. Sorry. I'm not much good with words, and I've wanted to say this to you for ages, but always been too scared, that you might think me an idiot or something, but I just had to, before I go, so that you'll remember. I think –' he falters, and the ladder trembles a little – 'I think you're pretty cool, and I really like you and stuff, and I wondered if, you know, when I come back at Christmas or whenever, we might see each other, you know, like as friends maybe at first, just to see, you know, to see if we get on.'

The declaration has clearly exhausted him. You wonder about the words, about what to say to an eighteen-year-old paralysed with embarrassment. You speak with care.

'Roy,' you say, 'that's, that's really sweet. Nobody's ever done or said anything like that to me before. So yes, when you're back at Christmas let me know and we'll, you know, hang out a bit together.'

You reach out to pat his arm, which flinches as though you've given him an electric shock. He's clearly run out of words.

'Well, um, thanks. Thanks a lot. I'll be thinking of you.'

And he gives your hand a little squeeze in the darkness, and then he's gone, back down the ladder which he puts meticulously back in its place so that Dad won't know it's been moved, and then out the back gate and off down the path until he's out of sight.

*

The night is silent. There are no noises apart from the occasional fluttering of leaves in the trees, or a cat stalking rats in its nocturnal prowl. In the house nothing stirs, beyond the occasional creak of floorboards or doorframes as the building cools and settles. In the bedroom a figure lies still under the duvet, dealing with the flow and retreat of sensations. Slowly it shifts onto its side, curls into a foetal position, and lets out a low moan of grief. There is this time no holding back, wave upon wave of sorrow, a noise like a tidal surge of desolation running swiftly, in the dark, through the house and out into the night, flooding the distance with its raw despair.

Over by Christmas

I want to make it clear right from the start that I'm not taking sides here. It's a very simple story, that happened a long time ago now, thirty years ago if it's a day, but somebody should record it before it disappears into the past, and I'm the only one around here left from the old days, or at least it often seems that way to me when I look around the church on Sunday mornings, or up and down the high street. Old people die, young ones move away, and in any case the village today isn't what it was back then, what with the new estate being built and the ring road. It isn't just about her, either, though obviously there wouldn't have been any story without her. Well, without both of them, if I'm honest.

I really don't know why it haunts me so much, this tale. A silly teenage girl wrapped up in her fantasies and a bitter old lady who obviously spent too much of her time cultivating resentments and slights – that's all it was, though it split our community for years, and left the parish church divided. And yet although it's easy to make a kind of moral tale out of all this, it's the loose ends, the mess left over, that keeps coming back to mind in the middle of the night when the past, rather than my gammy knee, seeps in to disturb the present, and not even getting up to make a pot of tea can help me find any rest again before morning.

It came to a head in the run up to Christmas 1992, as it inevitably would, but the signs were there long before that. In fact, I often think that if Father Peter had handled things differently earlier on, everything might have been settled sooner, without all the bitterness and upset. But he insisted on keeping open the possibility that Sally was telling the truth, when almost the whole village had made its mind up months before. Miss Vickers was just the one who gave voice to what they were all saying, behind closed doors, or in the pub, or the greengrocers, or finally, inevitably, in church.

Of course, if I hadn't fallen while rock climbing out on Windrow Edge and smashed my knee beyond reasonable repair, I know I wouldn't be part of this story at all. Back in my mid-twenties the appeal of moving out of London to the practice here in the village, where I figured I could escape from the surgery and spend all my free daylight hours climbing on the fells, meant that the life of this particular rural GP could hardly be more perfect. But after the injury, I knew I'd never be able to climb like I used to, and I started looking around for something else to fill the void. I'd been attending the village church often enough in the months before my fall to be on friendly terms with almost everyone. I don't think I would have said it was a matter of faith, back in those days. It just seemed like the best plan for getting to know my way around such a small community, and besides, GPs are part of the establishment – or at least they were back then – so I belonged there, alongside the headmaster of Windrow C of E Primary, and the bank manager, and Sir Clifford up at Windrow Hall. But after the fall, the church took up more and more of my life, so I had an inside view, if you like, as it all went wrong.

I'd always had a good baritone voice, and church choirs tend to be crying out for men, so I found myself at St. Oswald's more than perhaps the average parishioner would have done. Three services on Sunday, a midweek sung Evensong, and many other special services on high days and holy days, meant that I quickly became a fixture in the choir stalls, and inevitably in other areas of the church's social and political life. Stints on the PCC, chairing committees, promoting fundraising and leading appeals where a letter signed by your family doctor on church-headed paper might carry a certain weight in many homes – these things absorbed my attention and became how I defined my life when London friends asked why I wasn't dying of boredom out in the sticks. I don't think I ever thought about the actual, shall we say, supernatural meaning of the words when I sang the creed or took communion. But I saw myself as part of a living community that had existed on this spot since St. Oswald's was built back in the 11th century, and, in some inarticulate way, I felt that I belonged. But belonging, as I came to see, gets harder when one is pushed to take sides.

I first became aware of Sally as an individual, as opposed to simply as a kid whose mother I saw occasionally in my surgery, when she joined the church choir as a soprano about five years after I began living in the village. She must have been about eleven then, but with an exceptional soaring soprano voice that even in those early days seemed to have no trace of childhood treble about it. She quickly became a mainstay of the choir, whether illuminating the melody line in the familiar Dyson or Stanford (works which we performed with what I came to see as dreary regularity), or taking a nerveless solo role in extracts from Stainer's *Crucifixion* or Handel's *Messiah*. In her early teens she seemed to be always at church, singing, leading a Sunday School group, at prayer meetings and bible studies. Perhaps there's little else to do in a village of only five thousand people, but it seemed that church was the only thing in her life. It seemed.

When Ruth, who shared the practice with me, came to see me at the end of surgery early one Friday evening in June, and slumped down in the chair opposite me, I couldn't have expected what was to follow. After the usual end-of-the-week expressions of weariness, she made an obvious switch into something more serious.

'Sally Myerscough,' she said. 'What do you know of her?'

I reflected. 'Nice girl. Happy, even-tempered. Stable home life, as far as I know. Glorious singing voice. Holds the young people's group together at St. Oswald's. Why?'

'Well,' said Ruth, carefully. 'What would you say if I told you she was pregnant?'

'Bloody hell. No, surely not. What is she, fourteen?'

'Fifteen, just,' said Ruth. 'And yes, she surely is. Been in my surgery this afternoon, complaining of missed periods. We went through the usual options, and I thought we should do a pregnancy test, just to rule things out, and what do you know?'

'What did she say?'

'That's the thing,' said Ruth. 'I thought she'd be horrified, or at least embarrassed. But she just kind of smiled this secret sort of inward smile, and said nothing much.'

'It's probably just shock,' I said. 'Wait till it sinks in. Did she say who the father was?'

'This is where it gets weirder,' she said. 'Sally told me she'd never had sex. I know, I know, probably just in denial. But look. She's still, as the textbooks quaintly say, intact. And yes, I know that doesn't actually mean she has to be a virgin, but what are the odds? And more to the point, what do we do?'

I looked back over the complete uselessness of, by now, ten years of experience of general practice, and settled for what I hoped was common sense.

'We talk to her, and, if we can, to her mum. We prepare them for the fact that social services will need to be involved, and, possibly, the police. And we wait and see.'

That Sunday I took careful note of Miss Myers as she sang her way through the church service. She had the look of someone quietly, serenely happy. If she was faking it, her acting skills were exceptional.

It was near the end of the following week that I got a call from Father Peter, asking if I'd drop in at the vicarage on my way home from work. This was nothing unusual. We were in lengthy negotiation with the Church Commissioners about a grant for some major building renovation, and I expected to have to cast my eye over a batch of letters and reports. But it wasn't that at all. He got straight to the point.

'I'm about to do something I've never done in twenty years of being a parish priest,' he said, looking at me anxiously over his spectacles. 'I'm about to break the confidences shared with me by one of my flock. But I need to know that what I'm planning to do is the right thing, which is where you come in.'

He told me Sally had been to see him the day before, to tell him that she was pregnant, that he'd waited for her to tell him more, and that she'd referred him to Luke's Gospel, Chapter 1.

'I am the Lord's servant,' she'd told him, 'May it be to me as he has said.'

Father Peter put down his spectacles, and pressed his hands over his eyes.

'And what now?' he asked me.

'You surely don't believe her?' I asked, incredulous.

'I don't know what I believe,' he said, helplessly. 'Of course, common sense says she's caught up in some sort of fantasy, and probably it's the excuse to cover something far more sordid. But look, in every service that I take I articulate precisely this narrative, without blinking, and the good people in the congregation repeat it with me. If it's happening again, here in Windrow, who am I to deny its possibility?'

There was little more to say, but over the weeks that followed we weren't the only ones to take an interest in

Sally's well-being. She maintained to Ruth the story that she'd told Father Peter, despite Ruth's obvious professional scepticism. Father Peter himself seemed more inclined to take her at her word, for the time being at least. But the physical fact of her pregnancy went from unspoken sidelong glance to whispered aside to the subject of regularly updated conversation. Sally sailed serenely on, meeting the cruelties of school and the ostracism of some members of the congregation with her gaze settled abstractly somewhere in the future. But the village, that primitive and almost tribal organism, was tearing itself in two.

Every church has a Miss Vickers, it seems. It would be cruel to label her simply a sour and shrivelled spinster, which would be to take no notice of the tragedies of her life, including the deaths of two fiancés during the 1939-45 war. But with every passing year she became more and more desiccated, a self-appointed guardian of the church's traditions and narrowly-prescribed morality. When Sally's pregnancy moved from speculative rumour to visible fact, Miss Vickers used her place on the church council to decry slipping standards in sexual morality, to pronounce that the church must not be overtly seen to condone sin, and to demand that Father Peter take a stand against corruption within the very walls of St. Oswald's.

I recoiled from her positively Old Testament venom, but I couldn't see how Father Peter could let the situation fester without doing irreparable damage to our community. Looking at Miss Vickers, though her body was dressed in its familiar sombre black garb, her wizened features were alive, her face flushed with agitation, as though the exhilaration sustained her. Father Peter spoke of compassion, revisited his sermon about the woman taken in adultery, saying pointedly, 'He who is without sin among you, let him cast the first stone', but there was no denying that Miss Vickers had her weapons to hand, and would readily use them. And in any case, Sally showed no interest in playing the adulteress's part.

Ruth, who had no curiosity about church affairs, consoled me as the nights grew darker and the year headed towards its end.

'Look on the bright side,' she said. 'It'll all be over by Christmas.'

'How so?' I asked.

'Her due date is December 25th, which is kind of fitting, I guess,' she smiled, grimly. 'She's doing very well, in terms of her health, but I'm amazed that all this stress isn't harming her on some level. I've advised her and her mother to go and spend some time with family somewhere, but they seem determined to stay here and see it through.'

In the church calendar, the activities of Advent occupied a substantial place, but even the planning for the tree festival, the Christingle service, the carol service, special events for Christmas Eve and Christmas Day – all these were overshadowed by the visceral drama unfolding in our midst. Foolishly, I thought, Father Peter insisted on the full choir being involved in the carol service, with solo roles for the best singers.

And so it was that Sally, well into her ninth month, sang the first verse of 'Once in Royal David's City' at the start of the service, though the muttering in the body of the church itself sent a rustling round the whole congregation like hailstones against the transept window. There was some further disturbance during 'O Come, All Ye Faithful', especially the second verse, and the line 'Lo! He abhors not the Virgin's womb'. But order broke down entirely with the next item. Sally had a solo verse in the medieval carol 'Tomorrow Shall Be My Dancing Day', and as her pure artless voice soared over the wordless harmonies of the other parts, declaring 'O, my love, O, my love, my love, my love, This have I done for my true love,' I was aware that there were movements around the church in the dim candlelight.

Miss Vickers, her taut heels clacking on the stone, forced her way to the crossing at the end of the nave, and stood quivering, her walking stick raised theatrically on high. The signal must have held everyone's attention for there was a moment of shocked silence, before Miss Vickers screamed 'Slut!' and spat directly at Sally. She turned and scuttled crab-like towards the far end of the church, through the great west door and out into the night. It took some time for peace to be restored. Sally seemed to have fainted, and I glimpsed her mother fretting over her and then helping her out of the door by the south transept. Father Peter made half-hearted efforts to pick up the threads of the service again, but it was quickly curtailed and nobody stayed for mince pies and mulled wine.

Thirty years later, I look back now on that tumultuous Christmas with sadness, obviously, but also with the understanding that it takes so little to break something, but such a lot to put it back together once more. I never saw Sally again. She and her mother went to stay with relatives in Scotland. Father Peter got news that she'd had a little boy, on Christmas Day, and that she'd called him Joshua, but after that the communication ceased, and the village turned its collective back on her, as though she'd never been there at all. Father Peter stayed in post for the best part of a year, but never really recovered from the conflict. When he left to take what seemed to be a minor, largely administrative post at a seminary up in the north-east, the congregation said its perfunctory farewells and waved him off with no real sense of regret. St. Oswald's still goes through the motions, and I've been part its life now for decades, but I can't pretend its role in the community is as vital as it once was.

I had one more encounter with Miss Vickers. After the events at the carol concert, she took her regular place at services throughout the Christmas period, stony-faced and flintily silent, but after that she stopped coming to church entirely. It was three months later that, as the 'on call' doctor, I got a request to go round to her house urgently. I found her on her deathbed, gaunt, shrunken still further, her face a hollow mask stretched over her skull. I tried to make her comfortable, but we both knew the end was close. Her eyes flashed fire once more, and she gripped my hand as I leant down to hear her words.

'I have no regrets, you know, none,' she whispered. 'I did nothing wrong.'

She lay back, exhausted by the effort, but with what might have been a triumphant smile. The next day she was dead.

I'm still not taking sides. But it's the mess, the cost in relationships, the tainting of that very human quality, love, that I regret, and which keeps me awake at night. Sally's young son must be thirty, by now. Is he waiting, somewhere, for the sign that will begin his own ministry amongst the broken lives here on earth? Or is that just one more fantasy like all the rest? I'd like to believe it, though my faith limps on crutches these days. But over by Christmas? I hope not.

Out of This World

I can hear Sir William long before the door to the main hall crashes open. I keep my eyes to the floor, concentrating on sweeping the ashes from the grate before embarking on re-lighting the wood fire. There is a pause, punctuated by oaths. Then he barks, 'You, stop grovelling there. Go and fetch my dreamer of a niece, and bring her here, now.'

I nod submissively, gather up my skirts and head out on my errand. I know already what the answer will be, and fear to be the bearer of the news. Making as little eye contact as possible, I address the space to the side of Sir William's head.

'And it please you, my Lord, my mistress is at prayer. She will be with you presently.'

By this time, Sir William has painstakingly removed one of his riding boots, which he hurls in my direction.

'Did I ask you what she was doing, hussy? I said bring her here, now. And some meat and wine, while you're about it.'

I busy myself in the kitchen, where once a cook and serving woman would have worked before the pestilence came upon us, carve some slices from the lamb remaining from yesterday's roast, hazard a guess that yesterday's bread will suffice if dunked in wine, pour out a generous goblet, and hope that in the meantime my mistress will have come to my aid. Happily, I can hear two voices, one loud and given to roaring, the other quiet, gentle, but persistent, and bring in the wooden board with the food laid out as carefully as my trembling hand would allow and a knife for him to eat with. He grunts his approval, kicking his other boot towards me and points with the knife for me to light the fire. I set the kindling alight with a flint, nurse the licking flames into life, then prop his boots by the fire to dry. Then I retire into the shadows at the back of the room, attentive but invisible. I listen. It matters not that I hear their conversation. I am nobody. In Sir William's world I may as well not exist.

'So, niece,' he says, between mouthfuls, 'what's this I hear? Shutting yourself away from the world like some idiot recluse? The times have driven you mad, is that it? What right have you to decide this plan?'

'I am thirty-four, coz,' my lady says. 'I have lived long in this world, too long, and I have known its griefs. I am weary of its travails, and would gladly find a place far from its sorrows.'

'And so you would lock yourself up, like some shrivelled spinster? I have a plan for you to marry, niece. You are not so far past childbearing that we cannot have a fruitful alliance to enrich the family name and, yes, the family coffers. You know the de Gascogne family, no doubt?'

He does not wait for any assenting voice.

'Robert de Gascogne has got fat on the wool trade, and looks for a wife to warm his bed and give him a child.'

He looks up, pointing at my mistress with the tip of the knife blade.

'And that, my niece, is you.'

'My lord is attentive to my needs,' my mistress says, quiet but stubborn. 'But you should know that my future is not mine to decide, nor' – she flashes a brief but proud glance at her uncle – 'in the gift of any man. The world has no charms that can woo me from my path. My showings demand of me a life of devotion.'

'Showings? Your showings? The frantic visions of an addled brain?' He spits the words out. 'The rantings of a madwoman from the depths of her grief? You do not need this cogitating solitude, niece. You need to be flat on your back in the marriage bed and feel the kicking of new life inside you. That will shake you out of this fancy.'

I cannot say I follow every turn of what ensues. At times, Sir William demands more wine. There is preparation to be done before my mistress takes her leave of the house on the morrow, which I try to busy myself with as unobtrusively as I can. But there is no mistaking Sir William's rage at his thwarted plans.

'Niece,' he says, 'you are a fool. You do not know your own mind, if you ever did. You will leave this house in the morning and accompany me to Cleve Hall, on Robert de Gascogne's Norfolk estate, where we will settle a contract for your marriage within the week.'

'My Lord,' says my mistress, 'I will indeed leave this house tomorrow, as you say, but it will be for a far shorter journey, for tomorrow I am to hear my Requiem Mass in preparation for my final journey.'

'You will do no such thing,' he roars. 'You should need no reminding that as head of this family you will do exactly as I tell you.'

'My Lord,' replies my mistress, calm as ever, but with a playfulness about the eyes that I recognise from years of companionship, 'I fear that I must remind you that I follow another and far greater master now, and if you have further questions about my conduct I must refer you to my Lord the Bishop of Ely, who has given permission for my enclosure. I have written to him, confirming my readiness to enter isolation, and my ability to support myself in that state for the poor remainder of my natural life. Of course, I will have no further need of this handsome property' – she casts an arm around at the shadows of the hall – 'which will pass into your hands once my position at St. Julian's is established. And now, my Lord, if you will forgive me, I must go and make my final preparations. Alice here' – she points at me – 'will furnish you with everything you may need for your overnight stay. I bid you goodnight, my Lord.'

With that, she bows respectfully and slips out of the hall and to her own humble chamber. I step forward, but before I can speak Sir William jams the point of the knife into the wooden table top with an oath. What seem like minutes pass. Finally he looks up from his reverie.

'What, you still here?' he asks me. 'Go, light a fire in the main bedroom, and prepare warm bedding for the night. Then go and attend on my fool of a niece, and entertain whatever fancies she might have dreamed up for herself.'

I nod, bow, and withdraw. It is completely dark when I make my candlelit way to my mistress' chamber. She is putting a paltry collection of simple clothes into a bag, along with some sacred texts which I am unable to read, but which I have seen her poring over for many an hour.

'Sit with me,' she says. 'Let me tell you something I have learned. My Lord did not say we would never have rough passage, or never be over-strained, or never be uncomfortable. But he did say we should never be overcome.'

She grasps my hand in the gloom.

'Oh, Alice,' she says. Her voice betrays a catch in her throat, which might become a sob were she to let it. 'Tomorrow John Deverell, Priest of St. Julian's, will administer the last rites to me. There will be prayers for my funeral. I did not ask for the Requiem Mass to be sung in my honour, but still I understand the choristers will provide that office. And then I shall be dead to this world. Don't weep, my girl. This is my chosen path. And what I have learned over these past years of struggle must be written down, that others may have comfort from the visions my Lord has privileged me to witness, and for that I need solitude and prayer.'

She goes to her bag, and pulls out an object which she places in my hand. I look at her, confused. She takes it from me, puts it on the palm of her own hand and raises it before my eyes.

'Do you not know what this is, Alice?' she asks.

'Ma'am, begging your pardon, I believe it to be a hazelnut. But...'

'And so it is,' she says. 'But look at it with the eye of understanding. I asked my Lord, "What may this be?", and He said, "It is all that is made". I tell you, Alice, I wondered for a long time about this, and what it might signify. I marvelled how it might last, for I thought it might suddenly have fallen into nothing because of its littleness. And I was answered in my understanding: It lasts and ever shall, for God loves it. And so have all things their beginning by the love of God.'

She stands, and hugs me.

'Understand this, Alice. In this little thing I saw three properties. The first is that God made it. The second that God loves it. And the third, that God keeps it. So do not be afraid about tomorrow,' she says.

In the morning I wake early, thinking to prepare my mistress' room with a fire for the last time, but when I get there she is already dressed, her paltry possessions packed neatly, and ready for her journey. It is not a long walk from the steps of this once grand dwelling, in which my mistress has lived in the years since the pestilence first struck and stole half the souls from our city, to the lych-gate that stands at the entrance to the churchyard of St. Julian's. There is scarcely time for the sun to begin its journey overhead or for the birds to offer their first songs for the day's blessing. But she is anxious for the journey to be over. I wonder that she can be so content, knowing where she is going. I feel as though it is I who should be reassuring her, not the other way round.

'Live gladly, Alice,' she says. 'God knows, this plague we have lived through has stolen so many of those who were close to us. My husband. My mother. My two little boys. And your own dear brother, Alice,' she says, grasping my hand. 'I myself was on the point of death more than once. But know this. As truly as God is our Father, God is also our Mother. And it is a Mother's love that sustains us. "All shall be well," my mother would say, as she sat me on her lap and cleaned the graze on my knee that had brought me to her in tears. "All shall be well. All manner of things." And so it shall, Alice.'

And now she is gone, enclosed behind that sealed door of the cell that adjoins the transept of the church. I still see her, of course. I bring her food, take away her dirty clothes and wash them, stop from time to time to share news of neighbours and the goings-on of the city. She joins in Mass from the window of her little space that looks out into the church itself. I watch her quietly sometimes, praying or contemplating, or writing urgently on the pages of manuscript that Prioress Edith of Carrow Abbey brings for her. I cannot wipe from my mind the vision of that day when, the funeral rites complete, she passed out of this world, as the rest of us know it, and into her cell. But I know, as people stop at the window of her enclosure and draw from her wisdom, that though the loss of my mistress is a grief to me, and also at times, I believe, to her too, all shall be well. All manner of things.

In the Deep Freeze

'You found *what*?' she asks. Her voice is incredulous. 'Not sure I understood all that. Take your time, Jackie, yeah?'

I take a deep breath and have another go.

'In mum's freezer, you know, that big chest freezer in the garage. In some plastic bags down one side, near where she keeps all those frozen meals she gets. Rats. Two of them. At least, I think they're rats. Hard to say, and' – I can feel my voice trembling as much as my hands holding the phone – 'and I didn't look very closely. But there was something else, too, in another bag. I think it was an owl. Oh, Ellen.'

My voice breaks, and I can feel the nausea rising in my throat again. What comes out is barely a croak.

'Ellen, what are we going to do?'

'You at home?'

I mumble a kind of choked assent.

'Right, listen Sis. I'll be over in half an hour, maybe less. Pour yourself a stiff drink, and try not to think about it.'

An hour later and the world is a less hysterical place, though still baffling. We talk about Mum, and what we know. Mum's getting old, and living on her own is getting harder. I suppose we expected she'd need more help with everyday stuff, meals and cleaning and shopping and that. And maybe, if we're unlucky, it'd all start to unravel a bit. We were ready for that. Trouble dressing herself. Forgetting to eat. Losing people's names, knowing what's real and what's not. But not this. A freezer full of dead animals. It's just sick.

'Look,' Ellen says, 'you see Mum lots more than I do.'

We exchange an unspoken look. We both know what that means.

'Has there been anything, you know, odd about her?'

'What, even more odd?' I ask, with a bitter laugh.

Mum has always been – what was it Dad used to say, before he decided he'd had enough and shacked up with his secretary from work? Your mum's always been a bit of a tough cookie. He could have said that again. Even people who like her find her hard going. I remember my English teacher, once I was in the sixth-form and old enough to understand adult ways, saying, 'My, she's a strong-willed woman, your mother.' But, God help us, there's a difference between lacking empathy or social skills and keeping animal corpses in your freezer.

'I mean recently,' says Ellen. 'You know, like being in her own world more than normal, or other kinds of odd habits. I don't know. Anything.'

I stare around me blankly, as though my kitchen might leave a coded message in the pile of washing up. It makes no sense. Where would Mum find a dead owl, let alone decide to put it in the freezer? I shake my head.

'I can't believe she'd do this. Not on her own, anyway. And she's always liked animals. Look, she gives so much a month to that animal charity that advertises on the telly with sad-eyed pictures of decrepit donkeys. She used to volunteer at the RSPCA charity shop until her knees started playing up. No, she could never have done this.'

'Well,' says Ellen. 'Has anything changed then? Is she going anywhere new these days, or meeting new people? Does she mention any names when she talks to you?'

I try not to show it, but guilt is building like an ocean swell inside me. I see Mum at least once a week, sometimes more, though I know the excuses I make to avoid it. Fact is, when she talks I don't really listen. I've mastered the art of guessing the right intonation for the 'Mmm' or 'Really?' that forms my expected part in our conversations. Mostly I look out of the window at the squirrels demolishing what's on the bird feeder. I'm not really listening. After all, I've heard it all before, so very many times. What she said when the woman tried to jump the queue ahead of her at the check-out. Why she's stopped going to the hairdressers down the arcade after that girl was rude to her. Why she's no longer having anything to do with my sister.

There's something, though. Something indistinct, on the edge of my consciousness, like the shadow of an object I can't quite see. Until suddenly I can. I'm there in the room with her, at least I am physically, even if my mind's elsewhere, and she's telling me about where she's been since I saw her last. Lots of it is the usual stuff – the post office, a bit of shopping at the corner shop that that Pakistani man owns, can't tell what he's saying but he always seems very polite, knows my name, says 'And how are you today, Mrs. Mellor?' But there's something new. Something out of the routine. I look up at Ellen, surprise, a tinge of fear too, rippling through me.

'You know that lunch club she's started going to?' I ask.

Ellen shrugs. Obviously she doesn't. Why should she? I start again.

'Must be a couple of months now. She's been going to a lunch club every Wednesday for, you know, lunch and stuff. Company. Board games and a bit of a singalong, I should imagine.'

The truth is, I don't know where it is, or who she goes with – probably a minibus picks her up, I'm guessing – because I haven't listened. But. But…

'Anyway,' I pick up the thread again. 'She talks about it when I go over to check she's taking her pills and stuff. I don't really listen' – I shoot an awkward glance at Ellen, but she shrugs again and smiles – 'I know I should. But anyway, she talks about the people there. It's the usual, you know, people she doesn't want to sit next to any more because of the way they eat their soup. All that. But there's a name. Someone she gets on with, comes up all the time. Vic, I think. Yes, that's right. Vic. Vic says this. Vic told me that. I was sitting next to Vic the other day. Oh God, Ellen. You don't think..?'

The blood washes out of me like water out of a drain, and then rushes back, roaring in my ears.

Ellen discards the pretence of being amused. I can see her knuckles gripping the table top. I can't stop myself. The pictures in my head unspool themselves without my help. I don't want to say it but I know I'm going to.

'What if it's him? You know, the dead stuff in the freezer? What if he's a nutter? What if – what if, you know, now it's an owl or a guinea pig or something and, and, then it might be Mum. Ellen,' the words tumble out like a childhood appeal, 'Ellen, what are we going to do?'

'Ring her.'

'What, now? Why?'

'See if she's ok. I don't know. Find some excuse. Maybe there's something you've lost and you wonder if you left it behind on Mum's kitchen table. Just ... make sure she's ok.'

A minute later and the abrupt call is over.

'She's fine. Just what you'd expect. "What are you ringing me up now for? You know I'm watching *Springwatch*."'

Ellen sits while I make us more tea and then we go round the same loop again. Does Mum know there are dead creatures in her freezer? If so, did she put them there herself? If she did, what's wrong with her, and how can we make her engage with the help she so obviously needs? If she didn't, does she know who did? Does she think this person has something wrong with them? Does she think he is a danger to her? The thought of a showdown with Mum fills neither of us with enthusiasm, but there's no other way to do it.

'We just have to go round there and talk to her,' I say, finally, when all other options have been exhausted.

'We?' Ellen asks. 'I don't think I'd get further than the front gate. Persona non grata, and all that. I've never asked, but I assume I've been written out of the will.'

I nod, briefly.

'Fraid so. Obviously, I'd hope there'll come a time when she's a bit more, well, a bit more amenable to changing her mind about things. Anyway,' I smile hollowly, 'I'd share it half and half with you after she's snuffed it.'

'Not the point,' Ellen says. 'At this moment in time, I've been frozen out. She won't talk to me. She won't listen if I talk to her. No, Jackie. This is down to you.'

For the first time in a long time, I wish I didn't live on my own. I think about the usefulness of a husband to stand beside me, or a child or two to dilute the pressure on me to face up to this. I wonder if that's why neither Ellen nor I have ever settled down with anyone. Having Mum and Dad, and then just Mum, as role models, it always felt safer to keep to one's own company. Until now.

'I'm not doing this on my own,' I say, firmly. 'You have to be there. We just have to find an excuse – a reason – for you to be there.' I reach across the table and squeeze her hand. 'Safety in numbers.'

It's been dark for a while when Ellen finally leaves. There is a plan. I have no confidence that it will work.

I sleep badly. There are dreams of dismemberment. Sometimes it's Mum being attacked with an axe. Sometimes, rather disturbingly, Mum has the axe and she's trapped Ellen in the corner of the living room with nowhere to go. Sometimes Mum isn't in the dream at all, and I'm being chased by a tall man called Vic (I know he's called Vic because his name is conveniently on his blood-spattered t-shirt) and I only wake myself up by screaming at the top of my voice.

Even being awake is little better. I keep going over and over in my mind the moment Ellen killed Mum's cat, and how it changed everything. No, 'killed' is wrong. The moment Ellen's mistake led to the cat's death. It was foolish of Ellen to leave the back door and the back gate open, after the number of times Mum went on about it before she took the odd decision to go on that Saga holiday. We'd never known Mum to go on holiday after Dad left, and certainly the thought of her being in the company of other people made no sense, but she did, and left Ellen to do the cat-sitting. And it was bad timing, if nothing worse, that she should turn up home in the taxi at just the moment that the cat streaked down the front drive, onto the road and met a glancing blow from that passing van. We never found out what Mum did with the corpse, but when she said, 'She's dead to me now,' it was obvious it was Ellen she was talking about. That was a year ago. She and Ellen have never spoken since. Mum holds on to her grudges like a dog with a favourite bone.

It's a grey and dismal morning when I ease open Mum's front gate and make my way up the path. The curtains are open in the living room, but oddly there's no sound of the television you can usually hear even though the windows are perpetually closed. I swallow, a knot tightening further in my throat. I reach in my bag for my door key, turn it in the lock and let myself in. I'm about to do the usual 'It's only me...' when I hear voices from inside. Not the TV. Not the radio either. These are live voices, and one of them is Mum's. Panic floods through me, and I burst through the living room door, shouting, 'Mum, it's all right, I'm here now, I'm here...'

Two faces turn towards me. One is Mum's, baffled and indignant in equal measure. The other belongs to a smiley grey-haired lady in a floral-patterned dress with lacy white frills at the neck and cuffs. I've never seen her before, and for a moment we stand in a frozen tableau of mutual astonishment. Then politeness takes over from surprise and I step forward, holding out my hand.

'Hi,' I say, conscious of dropping my voice to a more conventional level. 'I'm Jackie. I'm Mum's younger daughter.'

I glance at Mum, who, for once, seems taken aback – mostly, I think, because there's no expectation that I'm due to call. I look back at the floral woman, who has stood up now to greet me. She's tiny, cheerful, but with a strong, confident handshake.

'I'm Vic,' she says. I hope she can't sense me flinch, the sudden collision of worlds inside my head. 'Your mother says she's mentioned me to you. It's lovely to meet you.'

The handshake goes on for longer than is appropriate. I can think of nothing to say. It's Mum who saves me from gibbering like an idiot, though not with any newly-discovered social skills.

'What are you doing here?' she asks.

Before I can reply, there's a knock at the front door, and then Ellen barges into the room, braced for anything. It's some time before any of us rediscover the script.

'Ellen, it's...' I begin, but fail to get any further.

'Well,' says Vic, with an expansive sweep of the hand, 'how lovely. How very lovely to see all of you together. And for' – she presses her hands together, like a kind of prayer – 'such a grand unveiling. I hope you think I've done her justice.'

Mum looks daggers at Ellen, who raises her hands in self-defence, but wisely keeps her mouth shut. We sit, Mum in her usual chair, Ellen and I on the sofa, while Vic (oddly I think, given that she's the guest) stands, centre stage, in front of the little table that Mum has by the fireplace.

'Well, Mrs. Mellor,' she says, with a kind of theatrical pause (she must have a sideline in Am Dram, I think to myself), 'and what do you think?'

She steps to one side, and pulls aside a cloth that's been covering the little table. Under the cloth is a glass-domed tableau, a crouching creature poised for eternity, peering intently into the space beyond the glass. I realise with a thrill of horror that it's Mum's cat.

It's hard to say what happens next. There's a pause. I can't say how long it lasts. But at some point Mum is crying, Vic is proffering a lace-trimmed handkerchief, and Ellen and I sit open-mouthed, as though stuffed and mounted ourselves. It's Ellen who breaks the spell.

'So ... you're Vic?' she asks, shooting a little glance of accusation at me.

I look back blankly. How was I supposed to know that Vic was a small, very feminine woman and not some tall, axe-wielding psychopathic bloke?

'And,' she goes on, 'and what do you do?'

Vic's performance has a kind of self-deprecating modesty. 'Well, as you can see,' she says, gesturing at the cat, still poised intently under its glass, 'I try my hand at taxidermy. It's my husband's business, but I like to keep up to speed.'

She puts a hand gently on Mum's shoulder. Ellen and I gape; Mum would never have let us do such a thing. Vic is getting into her stride.

'I like to think,' she says, with another pat on Mum's shoulder, 'it's about preserving some happy memories.'

The rest of the morning is a blur. There's tea. Mum finds some biscuits, only slightly stale, from a cupboard in the kitchen. Vic shows us photographs on her phone of some of the work she's done. Nothing bigger than a cat. Mostly she seems to do birds, pet rodents, that sort of thing. The presence of mysterious creatures in Mum's deep freeze is explained – Vic was suddenly very busy and running out of storage space and a casual conversation at the lunch club with Mum did the rest. I'd like to say Mum laughed a little, though that wouldn't be true. But by the time Ellen and I get up to leave, Ellen and Mum manage a grudging handshake. A relationship not thawed, perhaps, but thawing.

The Night Shift

A love story?

'Bill, what is this?' She holds the fabric tentatively, as though keeping it at arm's length would be safer somehow. 'I know your family are bloody weird, but, hell, there are limits.'

Bill smiles. 'It's nothing, hon, nothing much anyway. Just an old family story. A tradition, if you like. All families have them.'

She looks at him, disbelieving. He shrugs. Clearly it isn't weird to him. He can't see why she is making such a fuss.

She tries again.

'Bill, this is 2023, not the depths of the dark ages. We're grown-ups. We've been together long enough to understand each other, to know what makes us tick. I'm marrying you, not centuries of family history.'

He spreads out his hands.

'It's just a tradition. It's always happened. Well, not always, obviously, but always, you know, for the last four hundred years or so. It's an heirloom, and it provides, well, you know, it provides an heir.'

'Bill, that's mad. You know it's mad. Heirs aren't "provided" by wearing some old' – she holds it up, wrinkling her nose in disgust – 'some old rag that's seen better days.'

She throws it down on the table, wiping her hands on her skirt. He snatches it up protectively.

'Hey, you shouldn't,' he says, 'you shouldn't do that. It's an heirloom. Mother wouldn't approve.'

He stands up, holding the material by the shoulders, inserting the padded coat-hanger and letting the fabric hang straight and even again, before gently folding it back into the box it has come from. He sits down, and looks back at her.

'Think about it, eh? We can talk about it later. Just don't dismiss it out of hand. OK? That's all. We can discuss it another time, when you've, when you've had, I don't know, when you've had time to consider it.'

He smiles, that winning innocent-small-boy smile she'd fallen for at the gallery. She smiles back. She can't help it. It is a sort of reflex. She lets her hand rest on his sleeve.

'Well, alright, we'll talk about it another time. But look, there's no way I'm wearing a disgusting old thing like that, not ever, and certainly not on my wedding night. We should get that straight right now.'

That puppy-dog twinkle in his eye again.

'Another time,' he says. 'Just don't dismiss it, that's all I'm asking.'

*

The announcement of the wedding of Ms. Grace Atherton (she's been very insistent on the 'Ms.') to the Hon. William Alexander Ponsonby McGillivray, heir to the Duke of Darlington and, incidentally, to a large tract of the Scottish highlands, not to mention a stately home in the wilds of Norfolk, appears in *The Times*, and Grace is duly inundated with congratulatory messages from friends and colleagues in the gallery world. She points out that since she and Bill have been living happily in his London town house for nearly two years now, the announcement isn't exactly life-changing, but more a kind of rubber-stamping of the way things are for the benefit of his family, who seem more, well, more 'stuck in the past', as she puts it to her girlfriends at a celebratory meal.

It may be the excitement of the occasion, it may be just the wine talking, but the eccentricities of the Darlington clan become a prominent topic of dinner-table conversation. Grace is more than willing to reveal the antiquated amenities of Darlington Hall, the rooms heated by two-bar electric fires apparently bought in the 1960s, the lumpy four-poster beds that simply cannot be replaced because once, back in 1834, William IV slept in one on his way north to Balmoral, and the antediluvian plumbing system which seems to require a noisy 25 minute wait for the cistern to refill after flushing the toilet.

'And, dear God, don't get me started on what they wear,' she says, although it's clear that she'll start anyway, whether invited to or not. 'You know, I can smell Bill's dad from two rooms away. He insists on wearing this tweed jacket that I swear could walk about on its own. You know, that bitter smell of stale sweat and too much time being weathered in the rain squalls of all those hunts and shoots and whatnot. And as for his mother and her godawful antique night shift...'

Several pairs of eyes around the table focus in on Grace, who is suddenly beginning to regret this mildly inebriated indiscretion, and conscious of breaking a promise to dear Bill not to mention any of the history of this venerable garment outside the family circle. After all, as he has said, the private customs of families of history and tradition should remain just that – private – and even though she knows that traditions in her own family stretch just far enough to encompass the fact that her dad likes to put a fiver on the Grand National every year, and that her mother is not to be phoned or otherwise interrupted during *Coronation Street*, Bill's familial heritage is altogether more complex and, no matter how you slice it, mired in the activities of several centuries past.

'Oh,' she says, 'it's nothing really...'

But it is, and, only minimally encouraged by Sally pouring her another glass of red, she lowers her voice to a conspiratorial whisper.

*

At Darlington Hall, some two weeks later, Bill and his tweedy father remain at the breakfast table, deep in discussion of culling pheasants or peasants or some such. Bill's mother has invited her – it feels like an instruction – to come upstairs, on the pretext of showing her a sketchbook of drawings made by Victoria (that's *the* Victoria) when she stayed at Darlington Hall once 'when but a gal', as Bill's mother puts it. Grace wishes there had been lessons at school in how to navigate situations such as this, but the local comp was better at how to feed a family of four on a budget or how to avoid unwanted sexually transmitted infections (were there any that *were* wanted, she had wondered at the time) than how to function when out of one's depth in the aristocratic circles of what her own mother has taken to calling 'Downton Abbey'.

Still, she has made appreciative noises about the royal pencil sketches and occasional water-colours, agreed on the basis of no personal experience that having stray wild boar in the garden makes a terrible mess of one's shrubbery, and is about to suggest re-joining the menfolk in their post-prandial conference – she catches herself using this sort of language with something of a shock, unable to decide whether this is parody or the insidious influence of the situation – when her future mother-in-law disappears briefly and returns carrying an ominously familiar box, which she opens with something of a ceremonial flourish.

'I believe, my dear, that my good William has already introduced you to this,' the Duchess says, reverently removing the greying and dubiously-stained garment from its packaging. She lays it out across a convenient chaise-longue, standing back to allow Grace to appreciate the full impression for herself.

'Yes,' says Grace, 'it's, erm, it's quite old, I believe.'

'There are records in the family dating back to 1622,' says the Duchess, matter-of-factly, as though it might be true of anyone's family and its documented archive of worn-out clothing. 'It was a gift to Lady Henrietta Stuart, on the occasion of her wedding to the then Duke of Darlington, from James I himself.'

There is a pause for the significance of this to imprint itself on Grace's mind, for the weight of history to rest on the fabric in front of her. The Duchess continues.

'Lady Henrietta was blessed, as you know, with a son to give to the Duke, and thus she, in her turn, gave the night shift to her son's wife-to-be to wear on her wedding night, and so' – she beams at Grace with the certainty of the divine order being fulfilled – 'and so it has become a tradition in the family over the eighteen generations since, that the wife of the eldest son should wear the royal night shift on their wedding night, thus ensuring the continuation of the family line.'

There is a pause, a longer one than might perhaps be considered polite. The truth is, Grace has no idea what, if anything, is the appropriate response. She considers pointing out that the act of procreation does not depend on sporting some archaic talisman for success to be achieved. She ponders treating the whole narrative as 'symbolic', as though nobody in their right mind would expect to sport a four-hundred-year-old several times worn night shirt on their wedding night, that it's not, one might venture, the most sexy of garments. None of these responses feels entirely appropriate. Grace remains silent.

'Well, my dear,' says the Duchess, in hushed tones, putting the garment back in its packaging and then pressing the result into Grace's hands with the sort of reverence that might have been suitable if it had been the Turin Shroud, 'now it's your turn. May the spirit of Lady Henrietta Stuart and all her good angels guide you, and' – she pats Grace on the arm and shares an almost conspiratorial smile – 'cause your union to be fruitful.'

Grace is silent still. There are no words. But only when the Duchess has made her progress downstairs and left Grace standing alone does she realise that she is clutching a box containing a four-hundred-year-old garment to her chest.

*

In due course, the wedding ceremony to celebrate the union of the McGillivray, Dukes of Darlington and Atherton families takes place with all the appropriate pomp and dignity one might imagine. Members of his family wear kilts and a piper leads the procession down the aisle, his arrival preceded only by the enveloping odour of sweat-marinated tweed. Minor royals are rumoured to be in attendance. The Oxford college chapel provides a backdrop of suitably timeless sophistication, not to mention draughts sufficient to cause Grace to get goose-bumps. It could just have been the excitement and, let's not downplay matters, the sheer joy of the occasion. Grace's father has hired a suit for the event which fits him almost convincingly. Her mother contrives not to drink too much sherry before the reception gets under way, and does not even make a scene when, later, she is found asleep on a bed of fur coats in the cloakroom. There are photographs in all the appropriate places and it is deemed the society wedding of the year so far, although as it's only February this seems to Grace to be jumping the gun somewhat.

That night, when all the drunken farewells have been said and all the doors shut and suitably locked to separate the newly married couple from the distractions of the outside world, Bill looks at his new bride with that familiar shy butter-wouldn't-melt smile, and they brush their teeth together in the ample expanse of the ancient college bathroom. Grace isn't nervous. She and Bill have been living together for long enough for his body to be familiar to her, and hers to him. At the start at least of their first night together as newly-weds, there are decisions to be made about what nightwear is appropriate for the two of them. One of them, it must be said in the interests of full disclosure and in the light of the enduring scrutiny of history, wears a four-hundred-year-old night shift. But which one? Ah, that would be telling.

Acknowledgements

The story 'Ayesha' was first published by Henshaw Press on its website www.henshawpress.co.uk (Oct 2019) and subsequently in its anthology of prizewinning stories 'Henshaw Four' (2021).
The stories 'Remember Me', 'UFO' and 'The Night Shift' have been published at different times on the Sheffield u3a website www.su3a.org.uk.

*

All of the stories in this collection were written initially for the Sheffield u3a Story Writers Group. Consequently my first thanks go to members of that group, past and present, who have furnished everyone in the group with titles for our monthly story writing and acted as a captive audience for a first semi-public reading of these pieces: Jane Barry, Margaret Briddon, Julian Fisher, Neil Graham, Sue Halpern, Jan Henry, Myra Kirkpatrick, Margaret Maxfield, Mary Ramsay and Lorraine Wickham.

*

I am fortunate to have a range of 'critical friends', who have read and commented on a number of these stories as they were redrafted, and my thanks go to them for their wise words and helpful observations: Steve Draper, Suzy Epstein, Martin Hill, Peter Machan, Chris McKiernan, Phil Read and Cath Sweetman.

*

My greatest debt is to my wife, Ann Page, who was the first to read all of these pieces, offer sage advice ('your sentences are too long') and proof-read the stories for publication. Without her encouragement none of this would have happened.

*

Finally, any errors, shortcomings or flaws in these stories are mine alone, and for those I take full responsibility.

Phil Parker - 2023

Milton Keynes UK
Ingram Content Group UK Ltd.
UKHW011521221223
434831UK00001B/5